EMBRACING PASSION: ADVENTURES OF A WOMAN

CHRISTY CUMBERLANDER WALKER

LIMITED EDITION ADVANCE COPY

NUMBER _____ OF _____

First and foremost I thank God. And once again, I thank the Magnificent 7, April, Tessie, Two, Willie, Leon, Shaun and MyShell. You are the best children a mother could have and your unwavering support and encouragement has meant more to me than I have words to say and you know I have a lot of words.

Emmanuel, thank you for sharing your home with me. I tried to do you proud.

Ella and Bill you are the epitome of the word sister and brother. Thank you cannot begin to cover how much I appreciate you. Connor, you once again captured in a cover what I feel as the author.

And to my muse, I miss you and I wish.....

Also by Christy Cumberlander Walker

Novels

Finding Passion: Confessions of a Fifty-year Old Runaway
Sensing Passion: Travels of a Fifty-Five Year Old Divorcee

Poetry

A Heart's Desire (with Tessie Johnson)

www.christycumberlanderwalker.com

ACKNOWLEDGMENTS

TO MY CHEERLEADERS, THANK YOU FOR MAKING ME CONTINUE SO YOU CAN SEE WHAT HAPPENS TO LYNN. THANK YOU ALSO FOR BEING SO HELPFUL AND SUPPORTIVE DURING THE MOVE. I MISS YOU ALL.

Contents

THE FAMILY THAT BINDS

When I first saw Alita, I thought she was a maid. When I met her I thought she was a murderer, out to murder me. Our meeting took place in a hotel room in Nashville, Tennessee. It was a room I was sharing with her husband. He was a percussionist then out practicing for the gig he would be playing later that night.

Alita woke me from a nap with a knock at the door, pulling me from a pleasant dream. I opened the door expecting to see a woman in a housekeeping uniform. Instead, there was Alita in a flowing purple-blue dress reeking of femininity, power, and confidence. Alita entered the room without being asked and made herself comfortable. Then she explained who she was, which is why I thought she was a murderer. Her explanation of her presence had me plotting on how to get her DNA under my nails so the police would know whom to look for after they found my mangled carcass.

She was a stunning woman somewhere between forty and sixty, with skin as black as the inside of ebony wood. She had the ability to command attention by her exotic aura. Alita's face was untouched by time, not showing a wrinkle or any signs of surgery with chocolate brown almond shaped eyes that missed nothing. Her smile started in her eyes and worked its way down to her lips, which were full and brought the word luscious to mind. Peaceful is how I would describe her if I were only allowed one word.

Her voice was a melody. She had a French accent mixing with an unknown native African tongue, the result being hypnotic. When she spoke, it sounded like a song, no discordant notes, every sound flowing smoothly from her lips. She had the type of voice that made you lean in closer so you wouldn't miss a sound coming from deep in her throat.

Alita's purpose for being in the hotel room I was sharing with her husband only increased the intrigue clinging to her presence. She came from Paris to Nashville at his request because her husband wanted her approval for the relationship he and I were going to have. He wanted her to prepare me for our time together. I was the only one unprepared for her appearance and the time the three of us would spend together still has the same ability to shock me as it does to make me smile.

Once Alita settled into the room, she removed a cigarette from a jeweled gold case. The lighter that appeared in her other hand illuminated the jewelry she was wearing as she cupped the fire to the cigarette tip. Her inhale started the slow burn. I noticed one hand had gold rings on every finger. Each ring had brown, green, or red jewels. The other hand showcased silver rings with blue, pink, white, and purple stones. The stones winked in the combination of ceiling and cigarette lighting.

Each arm had bracelets set with the same stones as the rings on her fingers. Her necklace was different sized pieces of amber on a thick cord that nestled between her breasts. The multi-hued earrings that dangled and sparkled beneath her flowing dreadlocks were a webbed design. They reminded me of dream catchers I had come across in a Native American store. They had stone insets that created designs on the wall as the sunlight caught the colors. She was magnificent.

 "Mom, I asked everyone to come over, including Daddy because we're worried about you." Rene my twenty-nine year old and eldest daughter's voice gets through my reflective state loud enough to interrupt my Nashville memories. "It doesn't seem like you're even listening. How do you expect this intervention to work if you don't pay attention?"

It takes a minute to pull myself back from Nashville and Alita. I look around the room at my three adult daughters, mother, father, and ex husband Robert. They all came in response to Rene's urgent summons when she learned I will be traveling to France and Liberia, West Africa in three weeks.

Rene is tall and lithe like her father. She is also a fan of reality television. After years of living through her need to imitate television, I am ready to cut her cable line. Maybe the lack of cable will keep her from using the latest bullshit from half-ass networks to torment her friends and family, specifically me. These are shows where interventions and other personal business become substitutes for talent. Then the mishmash of trash is broadcast to the public at large and Rene in particular. Damn, this is going to be a long evening.

My father speaks from his position on the sofa beside my mother, leaning in closer to the center of the room. Retired military, his voice carries the tone of command. "Lynn I think this is ill-advised. You've been traveling too much. I'm, or rather your mother, I believe is worried Umph…"

My mother has elbows sharp enough to stop conversation. She puts them to use on her husband of over fifty years. I see the quick jab to the thigh and it has the desired effect.

"But we understand. Your mother is concerned and wants you to be careful." His statements ended, my father sits back on the couch. I know those words were not what he wanted to say. I look at my mother and we share a smile.

My father never owns an emotion. If he can't blame caring on my mother, he goes for bravado. I have long since accepted his need to be above his feelings because I know he loves me deeply. He was concerned enough during my recent divorce to give me money and pay my legal fees for accidentally stabbing Robert. Of course, he attributed the concern to my mother even telling me my mother wanted me to move back home at my advanced age of fifty-five so I would be safe. I don't know who would have been more horrified if I went back home, my mother, my father, or me. Parental love is great but it is possible to have too much of a good thing.

Rene starts droning on again. "But Mom…"

My mind returns to Nashville. Alita and I were discussing my relationship with her husband when he returned to the hotel room. Neither of them found the situation at all strange. Instead, Alita explained to me her purpose in coming to our room from Paris involved the concept of the elusive orgasm.

She shared with me the belief that certain people are able to connect on physical, spiritual and mental levels. It encompasses the two people building, binding, and forging a connection that lasts through life and lifetimes. This total, complete connection results in the two individuals achieving an ultimate sexual experience.

She then sought my permission for her to prepare me for my time with her husband. Her only stipulation was that I not come to Paris to see him as that would be deemed a sign of disrespect. It was a promise I freely gave. After all, I was married and could barely believe I had travelled to Nashville. I sure as hell had no plans on going to Paris. Then she went to work on us both.

Looking back it was definitely out of character for me to first run away with a strange man then to have his wife shave the hair off everywhere except my head. She rubbed me in heated oil-everywhere- and then dressed me so I could experience adultery with her husband- my only foray into unfaithfulness. She explained as she worked, that her ministrations would open our senses to the opportunity for complete and total release.

At the time it seemed right since I was having an all but physical affair with her husband. After she finished with her rituals he and I did have one hell of an affair. The kind that had me dreaming of him and his touch for the next five years.

"Ridiculous." Robert's voice cuts through the rest of the background chatter the occupants in my house were having..

I am pissed off I had to stop my reflections and I look around the room at the source of the outburst. Seeing my expression, Robert drops his head. I look at the others in the room to see if I missed anything important.

May, the twenty-seven year old middle child remains quietly seated next to her grandmother. She obviously has not made up her mind since she has not made a pronouncement. May likes to take time and carefully weigh her thoughts before sharing them. However, once she has made a proclamation she does not change or waiver in her thinking. She has a finely honed sense of right and wrong and does not budge once she decides to take a stance. She could stand a bit of humor to keep her from being so serious all of the time. But that's just my opinion.

Physically, May is a perfect combination of Robert and me and is in between the two extremes of our personality. May is not as rigid as Robert, but not as prone to spontaneity as I used to be before Robert and I got married. She is not as well rounded as I am or as toned as Robert.

"Now young lady," my father starts speaking before he gets caught in the ribs by an elbow from my mother. He starts coughing and I see a brief respite for me.

"Let me get you something to drink Dad." I toss over my shoulder as I bound up and head towards escape. Unfortunately, Robert follows me into the kitchen.

"Lynn what are you thinking? This is obviously a mid life crisis you're going through." Robert declares once the kitchen door closes.

"A mid life crisis is what I would have called your decision to leave me for the mixed animal print wearing tramp you're with now. But I'm so over you, I'd call this getting on with my life. It happens to include a trip overseas." I turn to look in the refrigerator to see what liquid refreshment is available for my father.

Robert grabs my arm and turns me to face him. The shock and surprise I feel shows on his face. Never during our marriage had he put a hand on me. Verbally and emotionally he had been a bastard but it had never crossed the physical line. Of course he never had to get physical. He understood my willingness never to risk incurring his displeasure. His total control over me was something he took for granted. I look down at his hand which he immediately drops under my gaze. My eyes travel up to his face.

Robert is a very well built piece of perfection. He still has a six pack most women and a few men stop and notice. With a full head of naturally black hair and smooth as silk apple butter brown skin, time has been good to him. He has a medium build and was the security of my life.

Robert and I met in college, and after turning me into a non-cursing, soft-spoken woman who allowed herself to be ruled by him, he decided I was just what he wanted in a wife. Then twenty-eight years and three children later, he decided we would no longer be a couple. His reason was because he met someone new and in his opinion, I no longer liked sex.

"Lynn, I'm sorry. I don't know what that was about. I guess it's my nerves. You've really changed and I don't like it one bit. You've been wearing different bras. That one you have on is not the white cotton ones you're supposed to wear. It's pink and I can actually see the color of it through you shirt. And it makes your breast look too, too, too, breasty. And I think I can see the outline of your nipple" he ends with a touch of wonder in his voice.

Of course he ignored my breasts for so long I can see why he is amazed. Maybe he forgot that I actually have nipples. Poor Robert. I could tell him the bra isn't what's making my breasts look too breasty. It's the skill of a wonderful breast enhancement doctor. The nipples added to the cost because I wanted them to be noticeable. They make me smile. If men can buy cars and get new girlfriends during their mid life, I can surely buy new breasts.

But it's none of his business. He left me for a slut who doesn't know better than to wear a leopard spot top with tiger stripe pants and a zebra print jacket. She dresses as if she has to wear all of her animals at one time because they cannot be left alone. I don't owe him any explanation about anything. He left me and I'm planning on leaving Wichita for a little while.

"Lynn, listen to what I'm telling you, doggone it."

"Robert, I think it's time for you to leave. I'm sorry the children thought you would have any impact on my decision. You don't. I intend to be on a plane in three weeks and if I'm extremely lucky, I'll have some adventures. Stop trying to influence my decision on this or anything else."

"You had better listen to me. You can't go running all over everywhere by yourself." His voice rises just a little and the look in his eyes shows the confusion he is feeling. I wouldn't be surprised if he stomps his foot.

My head tilts to the side and I smile at him. He is so transparent. His attempts to continue to rule me and my house even after getting a divorce are almost comedic.

"Well." Robert hems and haws.

I fold my arms and look pointedly at the door.

"I hope you won't live to regret this plan of yours," Robert says piously as he folds his hands in front of his waist.

"Allow me to doubt your sincerity. Robert, you hope I'll come running home after two days."

"Lynn, you should listen to what I'm telling you. It's for your own good and I know you don't know any better. You should listen to me. You can't go running all over everywhere by yourself." His voice rises just a little more.

"I think I've proven I can take care of myself. I'm not scared." The statement is not entirely true. But I'm willing to take the chance on traveling to see Paris, Alita and Africa, something I would never have dared to do six months earlier.

"Lynn don't make me keep talking to you. I said cut out this foolishness or else." He wags his finger in my direction and I'm sure now a foot stomp is imminent.

"Or else what? If I don't listen to you, will I have to get violent again?" I look over at the knives sticking invitingly up from the block of wood on the counter and within my arms reach. I turn back to the refrigerator.

In truth the only physical violence of our marriage occurred when he told me he wanted a divorce. I accidentally stabbed him in the arm. Then the fucking snitch, showing his true bastard colors, tried to use the incident as leverage to convince me to sign the divorce papers.

When that didn't work, Robert brought his new love to our home. He told me she would now be cooking dinner for him. I had to call in the big guns, my parents, to get through the experience. I'm not about to subjugate myself to him again.

"Get out Robert."

Robert goes through the kitchen door in the closest thing to a huff I have ever had the pleasure of seeing him exhibit. After he leaves, I lean against the counter to congratulate myself on my stance and gather my wits before getting juice, glasses, and various snacks to take into the roomful of family. I believe this is definitely going to be a long tortuous evening so I snag a bottle of white wine I had purchased from a winery in Indiana and put it in the refrigerator for later tonight. Just in case I'm right. Then I head back to the living room for more intervention. Whoever wrote the intervention rules should have told attendees to bring their own damn food.

Unfortunately, Robert is still here. I thought he would get the clue he is not welcome. He obviously still wants to dip his oar into the river of my life. There is a short break while everyone has refreshments.

I take my seat and think over my recent divorce. It was an extremely difficult time. I almost went out of my mind after accidentally stabbing Robert. I even sought therapy although it was more to convince the judge in the stabbing incident I was remorseful. My cold fish of a therapist left me even more depressed and potentially on my way to becoming addicted to prescription medication.

"Mom, I think you ought to go."

Lynette, the youngest at twenty-five pipes up after eating. I'm surprised she has decided to come. She is generally self-absorbed, but she is a rock you can depend on when she wants to be. Everyone except my mother looks at her with varying degrees of horror.

"Lynette, you don't know what you're saying," her father tells her.

My mother speaks up, "She's right. You should go; it will do you good to get away from here after everything you've been through." My mother looks over at Robert and sniffs. The disdain and insult she puts into a sniff is matched solely by the perfection she has achieved with rolling her eyes. Her eyes meets Roberts' eyes and she smiles before performing said eye roll for him.

"Mom, I have to agree with Rene on this. You have been quite a few places, but now you are going out of the country again. And to Africa. It's dangerous there. You could get malaria." May has not surprisingly joined the side advocating caution.

"That's right. And there's all of those half naked men. She could catch malaria," her father chimes in on an unwanted note.

"May, sweetheart you may be right but it's dangerous here too. Besides, Robert, you don't have to worry about me getting malaria. Half naked men do not spread malaria. Whole naked men don't spread malaria either."

I hear the deep intake of air from my father and look over to see my mother busy fanning him with a piece of paper. There is a tinge of red in his brown skin and his mouth is hanging open. Darn. Dad doesn't like talking about personal issues. Nakedness is definitely a personal issue and taboo, even though I am not the one who brought it up.

"I promise I'll keep in close contact. I'll send an e-mail out every three or four days and let you know where I am and what I'm doing." I want them to be okay with this, to give their blessing for me to go and don't want them worrying about me. If I don't go, I am going to be so pissed off.

"You don't get malaria from being naked. Heck, she could be in an orgy and still not get malaria. Sorry for my language grandpa," May turns to throw these words over her shoulder after hearing another intake of breath and seeing my mother fan with renewed vigor. "You get it from mosquito bites."

"Well, it obviously didn't kill all the people in Liberia, so I'll take some mosquito spray. I don't want you to worry; I just need to get away."

Hey. Wait a minute. I'm a grown ass woman. I understand the reason my family is concerned. I am not a goer and neither are they. We are almost pathetic in how limited our movements are outside of Wichita. My children have never been more than ten miles from Wichita except for car trips Robert and I took them on when they were younger.

My only attempt to leave my comfort zone before going through the divorce was to go to Europe. None of my family knows I never made it out off the continent of North America. Instead, I went on a two week tour with a percussionist I met on the plane to New York. Mr. M.O.P., (Man On Plane), Alita's husband.

At my lowest point during the divorce process Alita's husband's ghost helped me to get through my depression. With his encouragement, I went around the country learning lessons and kissing frogs. Through those travels I found the strength and ability to stand for myself and be a single woman after practically thirty years of marriage. As much as it helped, it also hurt because it brought me back into wanting him even though he is dead. He died onstage in Vancouver two years ago.

"But Mom," Rene whines, "I'll miss you."

"I'll miss you too. I'll miss all of you but my mind is made up."

How long does it take these interventions to wind down? Everyone has had their say and it looks like I am winning. Now if they would only leave I could review my list of what I need to pack. I look at my mother and give her my help me smile. She is a gem and starts the goodbye's rocking.

"Well I guess it's settled Lynn. You'll be leaving soon and we can look forward to hearing from you at least once a week by phone or e-mail. I think it would be most helpful if you call once a week so we know a hacker hasn't taken your identity."

I don't have to look far to know from whom I inherited my paranoia. Why my mother thinks a hacker would steal my identity and then take the time to send e-mails back to my family is a mystery.

"Sure Mom. I can try to do that. I'll call somebody each week or send an e-mail to someone and they can relay the message to everyone. How would that be for keeping in touch?" I look around the room at the rest of the family. My daughters are nodding their heads in agreement. Robert stands with his arms folded and my father takes my mother's hand in his. She rubs his arm with her free hand and they share a smile.

Robert has one more comment. "I'm still not convinced. Africa is a third world country."

"Africa is a continent not a country," I inform him.

"You know what I mean. The thing is you aren't a third world kind of woman." He looks around at the others to garner support.

"Dad, I think Mom has made up her mind. If she e-mails and calls, what more could we ask," says Lynette.

Rene knows defeat when it slaps her in the face. "Yeah Dad. We have to be supportive of her during this time."

May speaks up, "She has to get on with her life like you have."

My mother and father remain silent.

"Well now that we've all agreed I get to make grown up decisions for myself, I really need to get ready for bed. Thank you all so much for coming." How do you politely tell your family to get the hell out of your home? I look over at my mother and she instantly gets the hint and renews her efforts.

"We'll have a family dinner at our house, Lynn, just you and the girls. Just family. What date did you plan on leaving?" Mom is asking as she is putting on her coat and all but sticking her tongue out at Robert.

"My flight leaves at two o'clock on the third. I have a stop in Boston and then I have an overnight to Paris.

Everyone starts gathering purses or pulling out keys except for Robert. "Lynn, can I talk to you just a minute longer."

"I don't think that would be a good idea. We have nothing further to say and I'm sure you need to get home to Brenda."

"Lynn, I don't want you to leave. Maybe my relationship with Brenda was a mistake," Robert whispers as he turns his back to the others.

Those words stop me in my tracks. The children and my parents are too busy talking to hear our conversation. I'm glad because I know my eldest, and probably May, would be elated at this news. They told me during the divorce I should just wait on their father to come to his senses. At that time, I probably would have waited for him to come to his senses, but the hurt and betrayal have run deep.

I never expected to be facing my senior years single. I thought Robert and I would grow old together. We're not. He found a new love and showed himself to be an unfeeling, uncaring, asshole who would not hesitate to see me in jail if I tried to upset his new plans for our future. Now he is admitting he was wrong, but so what?

"What does that mean to me Robert? What are you saying?"

"I'm saying maybe I should come home. I'm saying maybe we should get back together."

"What?" My voice comes out in a screech. Everyone stops moving. I try to cover my outburst with laughter. "Oh Robert, you're so crazy. Why don't we talk about it later? It's really getting late and I need to get everything in order."

"Lynn can I come by and see you tomorrow?" Robert asks when everyone is again moving towards the door.

"I'll call you day after tomorrow. I'm trying hard to get things finished. I'll call you." I position him at the head of the pack to leave. I need time to think.

My mother hugs me on the way out then presses a piece of paper in my hand. "Just in case."

"Thanks Mom." I know from previous folded paper experience there is now a check in my hand for a surprising amount of money, drawn on an account in the name of my mother even though she had never worked a day in her life. She calls it her plan "B" money.

Lynette hugs me and whispers, "Let's have lunch before you leave."

"Okay."

Rene says "Mom you know I'm worried about you."

"I know Rene, I'll be fine. I promise."

May tells me, "I kind of envy you and I think I'm happy for you. I know you should go and clear you head, but I'll miss you."

"I know baby, I know. It'll be fine though."

Finally they are all out of the house I got in the divorce settlement. I think about what Robert said. I could have my old life back. Of course, it's different now because I no longer have a job, I got downsized with a wonderful severance package. And I would have to overlook how badly Robert treated me when he wanted to be out of my life. I could have it back.

The past months have been a combination of terror (of going to jail), sorrow (of losing my husband and the only job I ever had) and growth (from going around the country and finding strength within me). I could have it all back. Robert would be there to make the monthly menus for me to prepare and every other decision in my life.

I would have to take the pictures off the walls. Even have to give up potato bread and go back to the oatmeal flaxseed slices of softened cardboard Robert thinks is good for us. But I would have my husband back again. And Brenda, the husband stealing whore, would be sleeping single. Or at least sleeping without my husband.

I straighten up the living room, put the dishes in the dishwasher, and think about the carrot Robert is holding out. I remember my bottle of white wine and pour a glass. As I prepare to go upstairs with my wine, I have another thought. If Robert and I get back together, I would have to go back to not having food or beverages upstairs. Robert believes food should only be eaten in the kitchen. Decisions, decisions.

LEAVING WICHITA

The morning comes with all of the insecurities I thought I had conquered. I call my friend Dottie to test her thoughts on my possible reconciliation with Robert. She was my attorney during my recent brush with the law and represented me during the divorce.

"Dottie, Robert said he may want to come back home."

There is absolute silence on the other end until she asks the inevitable questions. "Home to your house? To live?"

"Yes, for us to be together again."

"What do you think about that, Lynn?"

"I don't know. I mean, I could have my life back. I could be a wife again."

"But on whose terms?"

"Well, we haven't talked it all through yet."

"I'm going to guess he told you this after he found out you were definitely going to be leaving the country."

"Yes, he did at the intervention last night. And he also admitted Brenda may have been a mistake."

"Lynn, do you remember what a wreck you were when he first told you about the divorce? For goodness sake you fucking stabbed him." Dottie has a potty mouth and doesn't mind using it.

"I know, but I could have my life back."

"And what a wonderful life it was," is her sarcastic reply. "Could you even go back to being that woman, no, that wife? The wife who had to prepare the meals her husband dictated whether she liked them or not?"

"I don't know I'm not sure. Maybe this trip is a mistake."

"Maybe it isn't. Why not go on your trip as you planned. You can decide when you get back what you want to do with Robert and having your wonderful old life back. At least until the next tramp tempts him."

"But Robert might change his mind."

"Would you be any worse off if he did?"

Her comments sound really negative. They are also brutally honest. If Robert would leave me for one bitch, he would leave me for another. I feel my strength returning.

"Probably not. Thanks Dottie. I needed to have my perspective checked."

"That's what friends are for, Lynn. I just want you to think carefully before you make any decision."

After grabbing a bite to eat, I head out for the shopping to complete my packing. I find almost everything in one store. The shirts I select are designed to show off what is now my best asset, a pair of breasts that make me want to keep my hands on them because they feel so good. I also buy a pair of tennis shoes. I haven't owned tennis shoes in over twenty years because Robert thinks grown women should not wear tennis shoes.

I get mosquito spray for malaria and sunscreen because the Liberian sun would cook me quickly. Alita shared we would be going into the interior of the country where they frown on women wearing pants so I get some sun dresses. I have to buy baby wipes with aloe and some pocket size packages of toilet paper in case nature calls while I am in the interior.

Alita suggested packing an overnight bag and a larger checked bag to accommodate the shopping I would do in France and Liberia. The plan is to spend some time in France and then go to Monrovia, the capital of Liberia before going into the interior of the country. She assured me it would be possible to have outfits made and buy something readymade for less than a few hundred dollars. Thanks to my mother and a wonderful severance package, money is not a problem.

I get some snacks, just in case I am stuck in the airport of any of the places I'm headed. It takes me all morning and most of the afternoon to complete my purchases. The final item on my list takes me to an office supply store to get a journal to record my travels. I am weighted down with bags by the time I finally head back home in the late afternoon.

When I get in the house and drop the bags in the hall, I head to the living room. The sofa offers the chance to take a load off my tired feet. The blinking from the answering machine gets my attention so I hit the button to see who would be calling me. Robert's voice comes through loud and peeved.

"Lynn I came by and you weren't home. I know you said we could talk tomorrow, but this is ridiculous. Why aren't you at home? Where are you? Call me as soon as you get this message."

As I listen to Robert's message, I feel slightly resentful he would go against my wishes and just show up. Then I remember how controlling he was during the course of our marriage. I never disagreed with anything Robert said. I never stood up for myself and my developing a backbone is new to us both. I push the delete button and advance to the next message.

The next call is from Harold, my old supervisor at the public relations firm where I was recently downsized. He has always been supportive and encouraging. Of course, I was a model employee. The downsizing surprised him but he recovered enough to plan on retiring to Florida. He offered to keep an eye out for another position when I told him I wasn't ready to stay home.

"Lynn, give me a call, I've got a lead on a job you might be interested in. There's a position with an acquaintance looking for a special assistant. You know him, Jonathan. He's over at Uster and McKinnon. You'd be great for it and they would start you off at more than you were making at your old job. He remembers you and thinks you'd fit."

Another job. Wow. If I wanted I could really have my old life back. It would be complete with Robert as my husband and me working as a special assistant at a public relations firm. It could be just as if the past months had never happened. Security has always meant the world to me. Robert's leaving and losing my job shattered everything I held dear.

Life with Robert was comfortable. I didn't have to make any decisions because he took care of everything. He made the menus, determined when we would get up and when we would go to bed. Since he's been gone, I am learning to fend for myself and make my own decisions. I could have it all again. This could be a sign. I dial Harold's number and he answers on the first ring.

"Hey, Lynn. Did you get my message?"

"Yes I got your message. What's going on Harold? What happened to Mykia? She's been there for years."

"Well she completed her graduate degree and decided she wants to leave town."

"Where is she going?"

"Atlanta and that's why Jonathan needs a new assistant. You're familiar with the ins and outs of the business so I recommended you."

"I appreciate the vote of confidence Harold, but I'm planning on going to France and Africa in the next couple of weeks. Do you think it will be open that long?"

"Probably. You could talk to him before you leave. Mykia will be there for the next three months, so there's no hurry. I told him I'd give you his number and you would call him if you are interested."

"Okay, what's the number?" It can't hurt to call.

Harold rattles off the contact information. "Oh and Lynn, I'll be leaving for Florida permanently in two months. I'd like us to at least have a meal before then."

"How about I call you when I get back?"

"You're going to France and Africa. Sounds like fun. You sure are changing. You haven't traveled this much since I've known you. Have a great time and I can't wait to hear about your trip when you get back. Maybe you can come down to Florida for a week or so."

"I may just take you up on your offer."

After I hang up, I consider how much getting a new job would mean to me. I don't really need to work since I can pay off my house with the severance package I received. Also, the settlement from Robert can keep me going until my retirement kicks in. With a little management, I could coast easily for the next five years. Or I could have a modicum of responsibility, a reason for getting up in the morning. It could be just like old times. I call the number and set up an appointment to meet with Jonathon when I return.

The next three messages are from Robert and I ignore them. When the task completed, I start to go upstairs. The ring of the telephone stops me before I can pick up the first bag from the hall.

"Hello."

"C'est va bien, mate."

"Hello Alita. What does C'est va bien mean?"

"It is a greeting, similar to good day. You will learn more when you come. Are you prepared?"

"I just finished some more shopping for my trip. I'm glad I made it here for your call."

"Ah dear one, do not over think or over pack. There is much shopping to be done here. You will not want to bring too much luggage. Paris is beautiful this time of year. When you come, we will also be going to Monaco."

"Monaco. What the heck will we do in Monaco? Isn't that where Grace Kelly lived?" This is turning into a much bigger trip than I expected.

"Oui. I have a little place in the mountains I think you will find relaxing. It is a spot I frequent to enjoy sensuality. I think you will enjoy the palace. It is a place for you to shed inhibitions, to embrace your sensual side."

"My sensual side. I don't think there is a sensual side."

"Of course you do. It just hasn't been fully explored."

"I don't know. Exploring my sensual side sounds a bit risqué for me."

"It is an opportunity. You may do as little or as much as you like. Whatever you do will be on your own terms."

It would be a shame to go all the way to France and NOT see Monaco is my next thought. "Well, I'm willing to go. I would like to see Monaco."

"You will enjoy your time and find growth and new adventures."

"Okay Alita. I'll see you soon."

"Au revoir."

"Au revoir," I repeat before hanging up. I gather my packages and head towards the stairs. Before my foot hits the bottom step the doorbell rings. I'm not expecting anyone and hesitate to open the door. It's late and I am a woman who lives alone. The bell rings again, with an intensity that gets me moving quickly to find out what is so important.

I look out of the window to see Robert preparing to put his finger on the buzzer yet again. How dare he come back here when he had specifically been asked to come tomorrow? I turn and actually have my hand on the doorknob when I remember I don't have to open my door if I don't want to open my door. I remove my hand from the doorknob and with determined steps, pick up my purchases and head towards the stairs. I go up, turn on the light in my bedroom and put my bags on the bed. All of the while accompanied by the sound of the doorbell.

The ring of the phone does not surprise me one bit. I pick up the cordless in the bedroom. Unsurprisingly Robert is on the other end.

"Lynn, I know you're home, don't you hear me ringing the doorbell?"

"Yes, I heard you. I even looked out of the window and saw you. But I told you I would talk to you tomorrow, not today. Why are you here?"

"I want to talk now."

"I don't. You can come by tomorrow and we can talk."

"But Lynn…"

"Bye, Robert."

I hang up the phone without waiting for his response. I look down at the phone in its cradle. Did I just do that? A smile starts and spreads across my face. Yes, I damn sure did. I do a little dance and hug myself before I stop in mid hug.

What if he changes his mind about wanting to get back together? What if I can't go back to his being the parent and me being the child? Have I grown too much already to get back in the box that was my previous life?

The phone stops me in mid step. The caller identification shows Robert is calling again. The phone continues to ring and I continue to look at it without answering. I don't want to talk right now. I need to have a clearer understanding of exactly what I want before having the conversation with him or it will be a repeat of the last twenty-eight years. Those years of our marriage were spent with me caving to him and burying myself in his desires.

In exchange, I had security. Robert made sure all of the bills were taken care of. He provided a home for me and our children in a well-to-do section of Wichita. We never wanted for anything. So what if he determined what type of car I would buy. He had done the research and knew which one was the safest.

He was careful about the way I dressed. He wanted me to look like a responsible woman at all times. He was probably right to tell me cursing was unbecoming to a woman. I found other ways to express myself that were acceptable.

Our routine sex was definitely nothing to write home about. Missionary style with no more than forty-five strokes to completion for him. Then I was on my own. But sex isn't everything. I knew exactly what to expect, and if I didn't get an orgasm, I could always get a doughnut.

I'd also have to cancel the plans for having each of the rooms painted a different color. When I returned, I was going to get painting estimates on having the bedroom walls blue, the living room walls pink and the kitchen walls yellow to replace the ivory and bone that is all over the house now. Calming colors, Robert says. I say boring as hell colors.

Plans on new furniture and dishes would have to be cancelled. The flowered couch we have had for the past six years looks the same as the first and every subsequent couch we have ever had. The sameness should be comfortable even though I hate the style and had planned on getting something in leather. I had planned to buy some blue dishes to replace the standard white ones. But, who really pays attention to dishes? You just eat off of them and wash them. Why fix it if it isn't broke.

Listening to my thoughts, I realize these are not my thoughts. They belong to Robert. Why should I change my plans because he has finally come to his senses? So I can keep my security? And for how long? Until the next slut comes along like Dottie mentioned? No. I am not going to make a decision about any of this until I have seen more of the world. I'll tell Robert tomorrow.

Instead of going to bed, I go to the closet and bring out my memory box. It has been in my bedroom since the divorce when I brought it out of the basement. It contains the mementos of my time with Alita's husband. I look at the items for a long time and decide that some things need to come with me.

I get out the red corset he had purchased for me in Vegas and promise myself to wear it in Monaco. Next I take the golden chains, as sinuous as water, and slip on the one for my waist. I also take out the Caesars Woman cologne and put it with the items waiting to be packed.

Bright and early the next morning the ringing of the doorbell brings me back to the world around me. I groggily grab my robe and head downstairs. Not surprisingly, it's Robert again. Brenda certainly has him on a long leash. Considering the way they got together, you'd think she would shorten it a bit. I open the door to my ex and my mouth to emit a yawn.

Robert starts talking as soon as his foot starts to cross the threshold. "Lynn, I think I need to have a key. Especially since you are going out of the country. This is ridiculous that I should have to ring the doorbell to get in to my own house."

I open the door wider and say, "Come on in Robert. Let's talk. But first, you should remember this is no longer your house. It's mine." The urge to slam the door is great.

"Lynn, I just want to be here for you." Robert reaches out to touch me.

I step back and around Robert to buy time. "Come into my living room." I lead the way as though he is a stranger. "Please have a seat. Now what do you want to talk about?" I ask as I settle onto the chair.

"Maybe I made a mistake." Robert looks lost. He has never admitted to making a mistake since I have known him.

"You said that the other night. 'Maybe you made a mistake'. Why would you say that?"

"Well it's Brenda. She doesn't cook the way you do, or fold my clothes the way you do or even be quiet when I tell her to be quiet. Brenda is not you and doesn't understand me like you do."

I think about this for a few minutes to make sure I am hearing him correctly. Is he really that fucking stupid to think what he just said is in some way a compliment to me?

"Let me get this straight Robert. If she could cook like I do, and fold clothes like I do or be quiet when you tell her to be quiet, things could be better between the two of you?"

"Exactly Lynn. You understand me so well." He reaches out again to touch me or pat my head like I was a good puppy.

"Hey Robert. Let's talk about this when I come back from my trip." My head is starting to hurt from the pressure and I feel my resolve to never do violence to a human being again quivering like Jell-O during an earthquake.

"That's what I'm telling you, Lynn. You don't need to go now. I'm coming home."

At one time I would have given his pronouncement the welcoming he believes it deserves. But not now.

"Robert, I plan on being on the plane in a few weeks. I would be more than willing to talk with you about this when I return. Right now I need to go finish shopping to round out my wardrobe."

"Lynn, pay attention. That's what I'm telling you. Don't waste your time and money going anywhere."

"It's not a waste of time or money. I'm going because I want to see some more of the world; I want to experience life somewhere besides Wichita. So for the last time, I'm going, Robert. Do you want to come with me?"

"No. Why would I want to leave Wichita? Everything we need is right here. And you need to stay right here where you belong."

"I'm not sure exactly where I belong. I'll make this trip, have some adventures and then decide."

"Lynn, you don't want me to get away. Someone else will snap me up in a second."

He is probably right. He looks real good for an almost sixty year old especially with the hint of gray at his temples. He was my king until he took me off his throne for Brenda.

"Someone might snap me up in a second too you know." Even though the fresh bloom of youth has long since wilted, I have brand new breasts with extra large nipples. They are perky even if I'm not. And they look great in a sweater and low cut tops.

"Yeah, right. No one wants you but me so let this foolishness go and let's get back together."

My wavering stops and my spine become as rigid as a mountain in Sedona. I look Robert in the eyes to tell him, "As I said, I plan on leaving soon. When I return, I will decide if I want you to be my husband again. If someone snatches you up before I get back, so be it. If we do get back together, it will be on my terms. Now if you will excuse me, I have last minute packing to complete before my trip. I won't be seeing you again before I leave. I would say give Brenda my best, but why lie. I don't like the bitch."

"Lynn, you are using really foul language. You didn't talk like that before."

"Robert, I'm practicing saying exactly what I want to say, in the language I want to use. If you remember, I used to curse, but you convinced me I shouldn't. Now if you don't want me to express exactly what I think of you and that bitch you're with you should leave. I'll decide when you can come to me again."

I walk toward the door and Robert has the sense to follow me. After he leaves I sit perfectly still for ten minutes to let the blood stop pounding in my ears. I refuse to allow Robert to have me unhappy about my decision. When my body feels normal again, it gets moving upstairs to finish packing.

Sunday I go to my parents for dinner with the girls and listen to all of the last minute warnings. Don't talk to strangers, don't make eye contact with anyone. My mother pulls me aside and tells me to call if I run out of money. Dad does the same.

On departure day I put a hold on the mail. The newspaper has not been delivered since the divorce. Funny, I am only now missing the daily information on what was going on in Wichita and the rest of the world. I call each of the children and my mother. Lynette agrees to stop by the house on a regular basis to make sure everything is okay and take off the messages from the answering machine. Rene will come and get any food left in the refrigerator. May promises to come by and start the car twice a week. Dad will cut the grass.

I close up my house and catch a taxi to the airport for the first leg of my adventure.

THE FIRST TIME I SAW PARIS

My flight to Boston is uneventful, with me in an aisle seat and no one chattering at me during the flight. The layover passes in a blur then it's time for the second leg of my journey. The plane is huge, three seats in the middle and two down each side. I wonder if my seat mate will be anywhere near as interesting as the lover I had met on a plane years before. Waiting in a side aisle seat, my thoughts remain on who will get the window. A young white scrawny looking male comes down the aisle.

"I'm here," he announces as though the plane could now take off.

He points to the seat beside me. I look at him and wonder if he expects me to bow or something. The thought of him climbing over me makes me get up and out into the aisle so he can get to his personal space that is way too close to me for my comfort. He is dressed in a tee shirt and plaid shorts even though the plane is cold. He has on tennis shoes with no socks and I'm sure his feet stink.

After he sits down, he turns, leans his head on the window and closes his eyes. We haven't even got close to being in the air. He must be high on crystal meth or something. I study him just in case I need to give information to the FBI when he starts acting crazy and wants to hijack the plane.

His long legs, sticking out from his shorts are hairy. Even at the bottom of his leg close to his feet, there is hair coming over the top of his shoes. The pale white skin on his legs comes through between the hairs like sunlight shining through the branches of trees in a forest.

My eyes continue up past the hairy thighs to the hands in his lap. The back of his hands are hairy as are his forearms. They match his upper arms, visible at the end of his shirt-sleeves. There's enough hair there to braid, even on his inner arm.

His face is as smooth as a baby's ass. There's not a mustache or even a shadow of a beard. No man hair is apparent on his face anywhere. Even his nose and ears do not have noticeable hair.

Not so with his neck. Instead, at the back of his head, where there should have been a delineation of head hair and neck, there is hair growth that continues into the collar of his shirt. The back of his shirt looks springy as if it is covering an afro. He should be comfortable on his hair mattress.

With my luck he'll have a weak bladder and spread the lice that are surely living on his hairy body. If he starts scratching, I'm asking to move. I proceed to be safe and reach into my purse and take out my scarf. I use it to tie my twisted hair in hopes it will slow the little bug incursion I know will be coming from him.

The flight crew announces it is time to turn everything off and fasten your seat belts. Mr. Hairy comes alive and goes to work trying hard to retrieve his seat belt from under my ample thigh without saying excuse me. When he claims the prize he looks smugly in my direction. I resist the impulse to ask him for the appropriate payment for feeling me up.

Laying my head back, I feel the humming sensation through my body signaling the engine starting. The anticipation brings a smile to my face as the plane moves backward then forward. The plane goes faster as it prepares to leave the ground and with every inch it moves I feel as though invisible shackles that had been holding me down are coming loose.

The plane continues to gain speed then tilts as air catches the wings. The air lifts the metal bird and holds it aloft and I am free. My ears pop once and then a few seconds later pop again before clogging. The fasten seat belt sign is on. I wish I had remembered to get the gum out of my purse, now stored securely under the seat in from of me.

As my ears continue to clog, I think about the man Alita and I shared. I was a slightly paranoid fifty year old going away from my husband and family for the first time. I had purchased a space on a tour to England, Scotland and Ireland.

On the journey, my seat mate was late getting on the plane. I was hoping the seat would be empty so I could put space between me and the guy to my left, my tour partner Hank. At the last minute, a medium height man with panther eyes of brown sprinkled with green approached my coveted space.

He wore a brown brim hat and walked as though he owned the airline. He started a conversation. I tried not to be a part of it, but he kept talking as if we were old friends. He believed we had met in past lives and were reconnecting in this life. I believed he was a possible serial killer who was going to sell me into white slavery if I wasn't careful.

Throughout our trip and at our layover in Atlanta, we cemented the bond between us. All during our seven hours travel time, he talked, touched, and swayed me as we flew into the heavens with the clouds as our floor. Almost at the end of our flight, he asked me to travel with him as he did gigs in various cities around the country. At the end of our flight to New York I had agreed to travel around with him for two weeks. He agreed to go with me to a tourist attraction in each city since I would be missing my tour.

I was amazed at my daring. I had never contemplated doing anything half as rash. Not for lack of opportunity, but because I was a married woman totally faithful to my marriage vows and satisfied with the security of my life. But with him there was that something, that attraction, that need to be with him. He said it was because of our connections in past lives. I don't know if I believe in past lives, I only know refusing the opportunity to be with him in this life was not an option for me.

Our time together ended and I went back to hearth and home. Mr. Man On the Plane, or Mr. M.O.P. as I thought of him, died onstage in Canada three years later. Even though he asked me to come and see him whenever he was in the United States I never went, except for once when he was playing close to Wichita. I didn't use the ticket he always left for me at the door and I left before the show was over. He sensed my presence on stage he told me in a voice message he left on my cell phone. I wanted to forget him and focus on the marriage that offered me the security I thought I needed. But I never forgot.

Then there was the divorce I finally accepted for the blessing it was. I had another otherworldly visit from him and my dreams continued. My last dream of him had me waking in tears. In it Mr.

M.O.P. told me to come and bury him in order to end us in this lifetime. He told me to call Alita so I would know what to do.

Now I'm going to Paris to connect with her. Then we will both travel to Africa for his false burial, an event I don't completely understand. However I have to go and end what is between her husband and me for this lifetime. Next lifetime, I'm looking for him as soon as I take my first breath. And at fifty-five, I am embracing what should be an adventure.

The plane is cold and I'm thankful I remembered to dress warmly in jeans and a shirt under a jacket with pockets deep enough to keep my hands warm. It stays cold until the manipulative airplane commandos, also known as the flight crew, want us to go to sleep. Then they warm it up a bit. I succumb to their demands and sleep, dreaming of a percussionist wearing a brown brim hat.

They let us sleep till it is the crack of dawn, then crank the air conditioning to twenty degrees. The nipples on my new breasts are pointy and poking the Sasquatch on my left when we both come awake. They could be hard because of the cold or the erotic dream I was having. Hairy man and I retreat from each other as far as we are able in our cramped confines.

Shortly after we wake up, they feed us a meal. The sun shining through the shades over the window is proof the daylight is burning and I will have a full day in the city of light when we get there.

Overhead the pilot announces, "Ladies and gentlemen look out the window on your left if you would like to see a spectacular view of Paris. We will soon be starting our descent. Please replace all overhead luggage and fasten your seatbelt."

I quickly grab my purse and snatch out my pack of gum while there is still a chance to keep my ears from closing. The first glimpse of Paris from the air leaves me unimpressed. I put a piece of gum in my mouth so my ears won't pop and watch our descent over the shoulder of the ape man. Green patches set apart by roads and houses could have been any city in America. And then we land and I'm in another country that is not attached to the United States. Let the adventure begin.

Coming off the plane is easy and navigating the Charles de Gaulle airport is easier than going through the tiny Wichita airport. Immigration doesn't ask me anything, just motions me right on into France. The French obviously don't take homeland security as seriously as America does.

Various signs point to where the luggage is being unloaded. Thankfully there is a monitor with the flight information in English to tell which luggage carousel mine will be coming out on. I breeze through the door and into a sea of people, some are holding signs with names, others are weighed down with flowers, and there is a group dressed in hula outfits. I try not to process the sight too deeply since a three hundred pound man, who has obviously not had a bit of sun, in a hula outfit could lead to blindness. I head to the baggage claim and get my suitcase then stand, unsure of what to do next.

"C'est va bien, mate."

I turn at the voice and greet my mate, the Liberian term given to women who share a husband. I'm not sure where I fit in the wife hierarchy. Mr. M.O.P. and I only had two weeks together, but Alita did accept me.

Alita embraces me before she steps back, takes my face in her hands and kisses both cheeks. She is dressed in a flowing black fabric and instantly enfolds me in her embrace. The perfume that wafts to my nostrils is reminiscent of the oil she had rubbed onto her husband and me years earlier. Her hands come down my arms and go instantly to my breasts. She openly feels them and laughs.

"Mon amie, you told me when we met in Nashville you were unhappy with your breasts. You have purchased ones more to your liking, non?"

I am speechless since she just felt me up in an airport in front of God and everybody. Then I find my voice to whisper. "Yes I got some new ones, but you just touched them in public, where everyone can see."

Her melodic laughter causes heads to turn. Her laughter is infectious, causing others to smile. She tosses her long dreadlocks, adorned with bells, shells, and gemstones and gestures with one arm, covered with gold bracelets and ending with gold rings on every finger, over the crowd. The other arm is covered with silver bracelets above fingers full of silver rings and hugs me close. "Dear one, you are in Paris."

I look around expecting people to be pointing, mothers covering the eyes of their children and security coming over to escort us to jail for indecent acts. But people are openly kissing and caressing all over the baggage claim/passenger pick-up area.

A handsome man appears and hoists my bag. Alita speaks to him then waves him off with a shooing motion. She causes stares because of her height and her ability to move with a grace dancers would die to emulate. People are looking appreciatively at her. Not surprisingly, they don't even see me. Except for one short round man who leers at my breasts.

"Come dear one we must travel to our home. Etienne will have the car in front by now." We head out to the front of the airport.

"Who is Etienne?" It isn't any of my business, but I am curious about the good looking man that has my luggage.

"Etienne is Etienne. He is for me as long as I care for him to be. When we are no longer for each other, we will go our separate ways. But until then we blend well together. We move in harmony for this time."

"Will he go to the false burial in Liberia with us?"

"No, that is not the place for him. Etienne is France. Liberia is different. The Grebo people would not understand. They would think I killed our husband to be with Etienne."

"They must know you loved your husband, Alita."

"We both loved him, Lynn. However, my people are quite rigid in their thinking."

"I didn't love him. I mean that isn't it. I mean he was married and so was I."

"There is no guilt in what you shared. Leave your western senses behind. If you did not love, why did you spend the time, why did you share the life with him?"

"It was the attraction. I couldn't do anything else."

"It was the chance to touch, to embrace the elusive. And it was wonderful. Do not denigrate what you shared. Look at it and use it for your future," Alita tells me with a hug before leading me out of the airport.

Etienne pulls a gold Mercedes in front of where we are standing and we climb into the back. We drive for half an hour with Alita explaining Paris all along the way with help from Etienne. Her accented English and flowing arms mix with his rich bass and are a great pick me up. Her words are as exciting as her personality as she explains what we will be doing over the next few days before we leave for Africa.

"Lynn we simply must go to Notre Dame for Mass."

Etienne tells me "You will be most impressed with the architecture. It is a magnificent structure."

 "Thank you both but I'm not Catholic. If I go to Mass, they might want me to confess."

 "No mind. We will go to Mass and then to the museum for the exhibit on music from your people, African American Jazz," Alita tells me.

"That sounds like fun. I'm not a jazz aficionado, but it'll be interesting to see how the music translates and is accepted here in Paris."

"On Monday and Tuesday we will relax around Paris then go to Cannes and Monaco. We will return on Friday and leave for Liberia on Saturday," Alita shares

"I hope I can keep up, you've certainly got an exciting visit planned for me."

"Surely you expected no less, oui? After all we are mates."

The car enters a wrought iron gate that opens at our approach. The driveway leads to the large two-story home tucked away outside of Paris. Etienne drives along the circular driveway to the front door. As soon as the car stops, a handsome man comes through the double wooden doors and down the stone stairway.

"That is Louis. He will attend to your needs," Alita explains at my questioning look.

Louis opens the door and assists us both from the car. He gets my luggage out of the trunk and looks at Alita.

"Put Lynn's things in the pink boudoir."

Louis disappears into the house as Alita, Etienne and I follow. The entry way is as big as my front room. It has a wooden sideboard in front of the window that looks out the front of the house. We go into a sitting room furnished with exquisite delicate pieces of white upholstered furniture on curved white legs.

A large gilded mirror is hung over the fireplace and objects d'art are casually placed around the room, some on pedestals, some on the carved mantle, and others on a glass shelf beside the French doors that lead to a dining room that will seat ten easily. The floor has oriental rugs on marble tile that reflect the lights from the Capadomonte chandelier.

On the wall opposite the fireplace is a life-size painting of Alita draped in flowing fabric that does little to hide her body. The red lace picks up the hues of her skin as it peeks through the open spaces of the fabric. She is walking out of the sea and the water clinging to her body shows as darker red on the material slightly covering her. Her foot is in mid stride with her head tossed back and her locks look as though her head had just stopped moving. The smile on her face makes you wonder what she just got finished doing in the water.

Next to her painting is a painting of the man we shared. He is also naked save for a drum, strategically placed. His legs are on either side and the view of his left ass cheek brings back memories. There are various drums and percussion instruments around him. The artist perfectly captured him in his passion. The power and movement lifelike enough you expect his hand that is raised over a conga to connect any second and sound a tone to reverberate in your insides as it passes through your ears to your toes.

I gingerly place myself on the chaise to the side of the fireplace so I can look at him without being obvious. Not because I care so much about him, but because it's a nice picture. And it is of him. Whoever painted it must be an expert or have an intimate knowledge of him to capture him so perfectly.

"How do you like the view of our husband?" Alita cuts through the pretense.

"Oh is that him? Nice painting."

Her throaty laughter makes me know she doesn't miss much.

"What made you decide to settle in Paris?" I ask as I try to drag my eyes away from the view that will surely haunt my dreams.

"It is close to the water which I love. Paris is a city of love, and I love. The people are accepting and life here is welcoming for artists. He loved the city with its rich culture. For me, it is conducive to my art."

"Are you an artist?"

"As you can see. I did the portrait of him you admire."

"Your work is very lifelike. I feel as if I touch this picture it would be as warm as his body" I tell her as I look at the painting again.

Etienne adds "Alita is modest. She is a well renowned artist and her work is much sought after. She now does commission work only, and turns down more commissions than she accepts."

"Oh. I didn't know."

"Etienne is effusive in his praise. The truth is I only paint what I feel. I refuse to paint what does not interest me. I am at the point in life where I paint to please myself."

Staring at the picture of him it is easy to see why her work would be coveted. I marshal my courage to ask her a question I didn't want to ask.

"Alita, since his death, do you miss him? That's stupid, what I mean is do you ever hallucinate and think he is still here?"

Etienne stands. "I will leave you to what is a private conversation. It is a pleasure to meet you Lynn." He takes my hand and gives it a squeeze, then bends low to hug Alita before leaving the room and closing the door behind him.

"Ah. So you have seen him since he is on his watch."

"No, he is dead. How could I see him?" I don't want to admit what I've been experiencing. She might think I'm crazy. "What do you mean?"

"Lynn, he has been here to see me and given your connection, I am sure the two of you have spent time. He told you to come and bury him and now you are here."

"Do you know all about what happened to me?"

"I have seen him. He told me you would call."

"So, what's going on and what can you tell me about the false burial?"

"Let me explain the concept of what you are going to experience in Liberia. A false burial is when the final change occurs. Our people believe when you die, you are on watch until three years pass. Then there is the false burial, the last farewell. Everything is over and you take the next journey of your existence marked by this most important ceremony.

"On the eve of the ceremony, the family will take off their black clothes and put on colors. The next morning, they will wear the best clothing they have. Food and drinks are served all day. There will be music playing, drumming, and dancing in the morning from six until nine. There will be another dance from three until six in the evening with horns and drums, the sound of the horns tell the story of the one gone before.

If the man was under twenty-five, the drums are beating and the dance is with male and female dancing together. If the man is over twenty-five the dance in the morning is by the women. The women will then dance wearing the yallowa on their ankles."

"What is yallowa or are you saying yellow?" I ask her.

"It is similar to an anklet. It is made of shells and tied to the ankle to make a noise as the wearer walks. The dancers will go through the village. There is much energy and the greater the person, the longer the dance. The dance in the evening is a war dance by the men. They dress in false faces with animal skin and cutlasses and other weapons. The dance is a demonstration of how the man would have fought as a warrior. I will tell you more later."

As Alita finishes her explanation, Louis with his tall copper color skin and hazel eyes comes to the doorway and stands. He is dressed in black slacks with loafers on his feet. He has on a sleeveless shirt that is unbuttoned to the chest and allows a view of a chest made for touching.

Alita acknowledges him with a slight nod before turning to me to say, "Come dear one, it is time for us to dine. I'm sure Louis has prepared something wonderful, he is so incredibly talented."

As she approaches him, he moves to the side for her to pass. She reaches out to lay a hand on his chest. He bends down and she lightly kisses both cheeks. We clear the door and he takes my arm to lead me to the dining room. Something tells me his services could extend far beyond the kitchen.

The room has a cream lace tablecloth over the long table. The sideboard holds large silver coffee and tea services along with various long and short stemmed wine glasses. There are assorted breads, cheeses, and wines with fruit and small plates. The soup tureen has steam coming out to mix with the tantalizing smells of more spices than have ever been smelled in my kitchen.

My plate is piled with bread and cheese to accompany the bowl of creamy soup that fulfills the promise of delicious. I eat and then notice my eyes must have been closed because I have to open them. Alita is smiling at me from across the table.

"Perhaps you should rest. We will have plenty of time to discuss events on tomorrow."

"I didn't realize how tired I was."

I follow her to what will be my bedroom for my stay. It is done in pinks and purples, with gold and silver. I would have thought so many colors together would appear garish, but not here. The blending of the shades created a lavish effect that is warm and welcoming.

The large bed dominating the center of the room looks inviting. My luggage stands off in the corner and my belongings are hanging in the open closet. My nightgown is draped across the foot of the bed and I am glad I had purchased new underwear for this trip. I didn't want to ask about my corset and push up bra but I feel slight warmth in my face at the idea of someone else, probably Louis, seeing them.

"Sleep well, we'll speak later."

"I'm sure I just need a quick nap. I'll see you in a little while"

"If it is to be."

Alita hugs me and then leaves. I put on my nightie and climb into the softness of the bed and under a throw for a rest. Before dozing off I remember I hadn't called to let everyone know my plane arrived safely. Tomorrow I'll ask about a telephone or computer.

Alita shakes me gently early the next morning. "Dear mate, the day is advancing and there is still more to do and see. We go to Notre Dame today. After, we will go to the Hamley Museum to see the exhibit on African American music."

Thankfully I brought some church clothes. I dress in a nice blue suit with navy pumps. Downstairs are coffee and croissants for breakfast. After practically inhaling them down, Etienne drives and our first stop is to pick up a friend of Alita's.

Deidre is a short woman with a round face. She has an infectious smile and greets me with a kiss on each cheek as she enters the car. She starts chatting in French and gets a blank stare from me in return. Alita speaks to her in rapid fire French and Deidre switches to English.

"Please call me Dee Dee. So glad you came to visit. You'll love Notre Dame."

"I hope so. Even though I'm not Catholic, it's church. How different can it be from the last time I went to worship?"

The short drive brings us to a bridge and on one side is the biggest cathedral I have ever seen. There are no churches in Wichita to compare to this place. People are milling about outside, taking pictures and being a part of the history of Notre Dame. Etienne drops us off and we walk along with hundreds of others lined up and entering the shrine.

It is smoky and impressive. The smell from centuries of incense invades my nostrils. With soaring ceilings and tall stained glass windows, it is a few football fields long and narrower than I thought it would be from the outside. Once Etienne arrives, we enter the sanctuary. There are hundreds of rows of folding chairs instead of pews.

Alita's friend Dee Dee is leading the way with Alita and Etienne behind her and me bringing up the rear. She decides to take the middle aisle to get us to our seats. Unfortunately, she keeps walking and walking closer and closer to the front, close enough to make me nervous. I am generally a back pew kind of gal. But like the energizer bunny, Dee Dee keeps going and going.

When we finally sit down we are close enough to the front to be altar boys. She obviously never heard of sitting near the back of the sanctuary so you can put up your two fingers as a show of respect and head out before the end of service. I am the last one to enter the row until a young lady quickly settles in beside me to keep me from running out.

Now on a good day, Mass is in Latin. So why did I think this was a good idea? I don't know. I look around to get a program so I'll know how long this lasts. The lady next to me has four programs. She isn't passing them along and the usher has moved up the aisle already.

"Pardon moi, S'il vous plais." I figure my limited French will at least get her attention. It doesn't. I try again a little louder. "Pardon moi, S'il vous plais"

She turns to look at me. I make the hand motions to ask for a program. I bend my fingers and put them together and act like I am opening a book. She turns back to the front of the sanctuary. Maybe I was using English gestures. I decide to point if I get her to look at me.

"Pardon moi, S'il vous plais," I start again.

She doesn't even look over at me. So I scoot over, give her a nudge, and point at the programs she is holding like the Holy Grail. She holds them even closer to her. I debate the wisdom of starting a fight for programs in the Notre Dame Cathedral. It could cause an international incident and I might be deported. I don't really need a program anyway. It's probably in French. But now I don't have anything but my memories to show I was here.

Mass goes on and on. We get up, we sit down we get up again and repeat the process until I think I'm on a seesaw. On the next sit down, we sit long enough for me to start drifting off to sleep.

"Let us leave," Alita whispers.

I couldn't agree more. I stand up and walk toward the aisle. The program hoarder lets out a breath and gives me a haughty look. I move my foot back so I can accidentally kick her on the way out. Alita touches me on my shoulder and I settle for stepping on Ms. Selfish Lady's foot instead. She emits a rather loud shriek and I hear smothered laughter behind me as I lead the processional from the sanctuary.

"We'll get something to eat at the Hard Rock Cafe, close to the museum. You will be able to order food you are used to eating," Alita says when we exit the church.

The Hard Rock Café is like a step back into the United States except for the French voices. The restaurant has a musical theme with videos playing of great musicians. The artwork throughout consists of instruments played by famous musicians all around the restaurant. Alita takes me to a set of hand drums. They belonged to him and were played when the fellows performed at the inauguration of the current president of France. We eat and talk with Alita promising to show me the sights of the city.

"We will go the museum today and then ride the train," Alita says.

Dee Dee says, "I think I'll just go back home. I am having visitors."

"Etienne would not mind taking you. Lynn and I will see Paris."

Alita and I walk a few blocks away and come to the museum with its exhibit on a century of jazz. I am faced with pictures of black people with tails, black people hanging on trees as Christmas ornaments, and pretty much every other racial stereotype I knew about and a bit more I was seeing for the first time.

I couldn't finish the exhibit after seeing the picture of the black male with slice of watermelon and a shit eating grin. I want to bust up the rest of this bullshit. Then it dawns on me they would probably put me away in a Parisian prison for a long time. And I had the little incident with the stabbing. I settle for leaving in disgust, determined to write a letter expressing my dissatisfaction with their exhibit of every racist denigration of African Americans they could find.

"Alita, you go ahead and see the exhibit. I'll meet you outside."

"Is something wrong?"

"I'm still tired from the trip. I'm fine."

Maybe I'm overly sensitive. I go out to the black iron mesh benches I had noticed on my way inside and sit, hoping a breeze will blow to cool me off. I'm heated after the exhibit in honor of racism these French assholes are holding up as realistic depiction of Black music in America. My foot is tapping and I am waving my program to give an outlet to some of the anger inside.

A concerned looking man with graying temples sits beside me. I look at him and roll my eyes. I'm not feeling Frenchies right now.

"Hi, how are you?" he asks in my kind of English. The American kind.

"I'm fine. Imagine meeting another American in Paris. Where are you from? "

"Iowa. I'm visiting Paris with my wife and wanted to see the African American music exhibit."

"That bunch of bull. I hated it. It was insulting and offensive and it pisses me off to think French people see us as humans with tails."

"Whoa there." He holds his hands in front of him.

"I can't help it. I saw more musical information at the Hard Rock café around the corner. At least they had video and the guitar of Jimi Hendrix. Did you see the pictures in that place?" I indicate the offensive museum with a backward jerk of my thumb.

"I've seen it several times and appreciate the historical significance."

"Why would you say something like that? If I had a museum with a French exhibit that depicted French people as snail eating frogs or their men as bisexual eunuchs and their women as perfumed whores who put rouge on their nipples, do you think they might be offended?"

"Um, probably," he agrees, "but this is different."

"How is it different? Are you a musician?"

"I used to play, but I also taught music for a number of years," he shares.

"Then I would appreciate if you could tell me three things about the exhibit, and I use the term exhibit loosely, that had any redeeming social value."

"Well, I think the curators had a lot of items they didn't know what to do with. They decided to just show it instead of showing it in context."

H has got to be kidding. "What could the context be?"

"What was happening in society when the music was being made. It was post Reconstruction and there was a backlash from the south. In a musical context, the images were approved ways to attack blacks. And then you had the blacks, who wanted to play the music their way. They took white traditional music and stood it on its head. The whites couldn't follow it so that led to a certain frustration," he explains.

"Then why didn't the musicians stop being the model for the stereotypes?"

"It would have meant the artists not playing. Many of them came to Paris where they were accepted, far more accepted than in the States" he explains.

"Do you think they were accepted because they were black or because there was just a few of them in the overall scheme of things and they were extremely talented?"

"Probably a bit of both. This would have been a much more effective exhibit if there had been more information about the times, but, hey, you take what you get."

"Well I'm surprised black Parisians aren't picketing this crap."

"They don't have our history. This could not have been shown in the same way in any city in America. The curators definitely would have included more contexts for the visitor, and then it could be appreciated."

When Alita comes out of the museum, she finds me with my new musical guide.

"Bon jour, Brian. How is your music?"

"Alita, it's been forever."

"I saw your wife inside. She said I would find you here. How long is your stay?" Alita asks

"We leave next week. I tried to call but Etienne said you were going to be traveling," Brian tells her.

"Yes, to Liberia for the false burial. I see you've met my mate, Lynn," Alita says by way of introduction.

Brian looks at me in surprise. "An American mate? How unusual."

"He was an unusual man." I tell him as I join their conversation.

"He was also a fantastic musician. I studied with him in Africa years ago." He turns to Alita to say, "I was explaining the exhibit to Lynn. She wasn't fond of the works and was very passionate about her thoughts."

"Yes. Lynn feels deeply." Alita agrees.

"Will the two of you join us for dinner before we leave? Patience and I would love the opportunity to visit. We're staying at the usual place," Brian says.

"Why not come to us for dinner? The fellows are in town and it will be nice to catch up and talk music," Alita replies.

"I'll ask Patience when she comes out. Thank you for inviting us," Brian accepts.

"Alita, I didn't know the other musicians in the band would be here. What are they doing in France?" I ask her.

"We often gather and remember him. They are on their way to a festival in England, so we will get together and reminisce. It will be nice to have the opportunity to visit before we leave for the false burial." Alita turns to Brian and continues, "I'll call this evening with details. Bon jour."

We leave Brian and Alita takes my hand to say, "Let us take a train so you can understand Paris. We will use it to go to home."

We get our ticket and board the underground rail system you cannot tell exists aboveground. The train ride begins pleasantly enough. A young man and younger looking woman board at the second stop. They have a big boom box the man puts to use almost immediately.

The woman starts singing and moving her body around the pole passengers are supposed to grasp onto when they are standing. She leans against it holding on more than anything else. She doesn't put much heart or energy into the movements.

Her lank, greasy, brown, hair comes to her shoulder and she tries to fling it, but it doesn't move. Her attempts to work the pole like a stripper are equally ineffective. The train keeps moving and must keep her off balance because she is holding on to the pole like it is a lifeline pulling her from the water.

She makes no attempt to lift her stiletto covered foot from the floor. This is a good thing since she is wobbling on them while both feet are on the floor. Her knobby knees and painted finger nails further the image of crack whore.

Then her pimp jumps up to the top of one pole and wraps his ankle around the top. He slowly gyrates down head first, no easy feat by my standards. When they finish their show, people throw money at the plastic bucket he holds in front of his chest. I am ready to throw a euro at him but with my luck, it would put his eye out. Thoughts of being in the dungeon of a damn Parisian prison stop me from tossing the coin. I keep my euro safely in my pocket and remove my hand.

It's good to know if times get hard I can always wrap my leg around a pole on a train in Paris. I wouldn't be the first black woman to dance in Paris. Josephine Baker comes to mind. After the wanna be dancer and her manager get off I hope my excitement is over.

But at the next stop, le Bourget, the train stops, the conductor says something I don't understand and then the train goes silent. Three guards with a big possibly drug sniffing dog are visible on the platform. Thankfully they find whatever they are looking for and it does not include me.

Once we leave the train a few stops later and make it to the top of the stairs, Etienne is there waiting for us with the car. We climb into the car and go home.

Louis lets us in and announces with the formality of the butler to the Queen of England, "Crepes with cream, chocolate and nut filling are prepared for your enjoyment." He smiles at me and takes my hand to lead me into the dining room. He gives my hand a squeeze before seating me at the table. I ask Alita to use her computer in order to send a message once we have finished the serving of heaven Louis served with a cup of coffee.

She takes me into her study. The room has pictures of African village scenes as well as French street scenes and pictures of Mr. M.O.P. the carved desk holding the computer is unique with the inlaid ivory scrolling down the front. The feet of the desk were carved and the pigeon hole section on the top of the desk had ornate double doors.

"Make this your home. Use the computer and anything else whenever you like."

"Is there a password?"

"There are no passwords. Passwords restrict. This is a home of freedom. Help yourself to whatever you see. I shall retire now."

What can I say about my time in Paris that will not make the family worry or be concerned? It makes sense to send the e-mail to my biggest supporter, my mother.

E-MAILS TO HOME

Hi Mom,

Here's a short recap of my trip so far.

On the plane over, I got felt up by Sasquatch, my seat mate. Everyone here is kissing or doing something more intense. I saw a pole dancer on the train. Don't worry about me turning Catholic.

Peace, Love and Frenchmen

Lynn

A WALK AROUND PARIS

"Lynn, Lynn, wake up. Today we walk around Paris. We will see the Tower, the writers' park, and other tourist sites. He said you like touristy so we will see the usual and we shall ride the funicular" Alita's excited voice gets me moving.

"I haven't been on a bicycle since I was in my teens. I don't think riding a funicular will be good for my knees. Old bones don't heal easily and I think a funicular is not for me. Besides, Alita, I'm not real sports minded."

 Alita has a puzzled look on her face then the look becomes a smile.

"Lynn, the funicular is like an elevator. It will take us up the mountain to see a view of the city. Come the daylight is burning. Wear some comfortable shoes." She leaves the room and her scent stays in the air, the smell of adventure

I dress in a lightweight skirt and some comfy shoes then head down for breakfast. The crepes are so light they would drift away without the bananas and whipped cream to keep them on the plate. I decline the coffee that is strong enough to move a mountain, and settle for a cup of hot chocolate Louis offers. Throughout the meal Alita continues to regale me with our agenda for the day.

Etienne brings the car around and we head into the heart of Paris.

"Etienne, you may pick us up at the Eiffel Tower in three hours," Alita commands as we exit the vehicle and enter the park where Alita starts my education of Paris.

"In the early 1800's, there was a mass migration of African Americans to France because bounty hunters could not return slaves to America. The migration continued and many expatriates came to live here. This park is where Langston Hughes and James Weldon Johnson often visited. Hughes is said to have lived in a top floor garret in the 1920's. W. E. B. Dubois was also here for a period of time."

We come to the statue of Alexander Dumas Alita tells me is the only statue dedicated to a black man in Paris. I look at the carvings of a young man, woman and old man surrounding the bottom of the statue.

"Alita, what do the figures symbolize."

"This shows the wide variety of people he appealed to with his art. As you are aware, he wrote novels. The thespian symbols, the happy and sad face, show he wrote plays. Few know he also wrote cookbooks. On the back of the statue is a carving of Dartanyan, the black musketeer."

The park is beautiful. Unfortunately, there are public displays of affection all over. Everybody here is kissing, fondling or otherwise engaged in close to the bedroom activity. The most blatant sight I observe outside and in public is a couples way too involved. He is almost on top of her. Her head is thrown back and when he finally opens his eyes, I know they both need a bath, the nasty bastards. I am watching intently until Alita clears her throat.

We continue on the park walkways and come to a busy intersection at the end of the street.

"The park has an unobstructed view of the Arch de Triumph." The structure is powerful. The curves and lines of the arch are a testament to architecture.

"Why is it called Arch de Triumph?"

"It was created in honor of the generals of Napoleon. The father of Alexander Dumas is among the names inscribed on the structure. The newest Parisian monument is named "Irons" for General Dumas. It is two shackles with separated chains." She shows off her city to me with a confidence I can only aspire to achieve.

"Perhaps you would like to see Salle Pleyel. It is the concert hall where Louis Armstrong and others played when they came to Paris. It was built by Salle Pleyel, a member of a family of piano makers. Recently, it has completed a renovation that lasted ten years."

We continue out of the park past the Arc and go to a lovely brick building. Black, cream, and taupe designs on the entry floor lead into a magnificent soaring stairway with red carpet and black railing. Mirrors flanking the walls give theatergoers the opportunity to preen. It isn't hard to imagine artists coming here to perform and if you listened you could probably hear the echoes of past masters, Duke Ellington, and others performing and strutting. The building houses a theater and restaurant.

"Alita, I don't understand how you have this magnificent concert hall where African Americans played, yet you accept the blatant racism from the museum exhibit."

"Racism? What do you mean racism?

"They way they showed black people, that didn't bother you?"

"I did not see what you saw. My eyes were focused on the music. But I have no doubt you will enjoy dinner with Brian and Patience."

From Salle Pleyel we go to a large white building at the bottom of a very steep mountain. We are in the midst of an area called Little Africa. The sights and sounds bombard the sense of smell and sight. Spices from who knows where compete with the foods being cooked and served up over rice or noodles in sauces with bread. There are fried pocket sandwiches and fresh peanuts. We wonder around and I enjoy the infusion of different cultures on my consciousness.

We eventually come to the funicular, a large glass elevator. People are standing shoulder to shoulder waiting to get on. Alita takes my hand so I don't get lost in the crowd. If I believe enough in physics, I'll get in and travel up the mountain. It doesn't look completely trustworthy, but Alita said there's never been a crash and no one else seems afraid. I get in.

The crowd soon pushes us apart and I have the rail in the front window. The doors close then open slightly. A tall gentleman hoisting a bicycle onto his shoulder enters before the doors close again and we begin our journey up the mountainside. Bicycle man soon wedges himself close to me and I can tell he's spent a while riding and lifting the bike by the size of the muscles shining through his Speedo's. His shorts also show he is extremely equipped to give a good ride if size matters. And I know it does. I turn my attention to where we are going.

As we ride up, there is the chattering of various languages, giving testimony to the international flavor of Paris. Again, everyone has someone to be happy with. From the young blond couple openly kissing to the two stooped gray haired couple holding arthritic hands as they smile at each other, everyone has someone. Paris is a city for romance and I got nobody. I look around when I feel a person touching my arm. It's Cycle Guy. I move slightly to the left and locate Alita. She is on the other side of the ride.

"Hello there. Are you new to Paris?" The man with the bike has an island accent to go with his wide face and an open smile. He is rather large, standing over six three. His clothes show he has a lot to be thankful for and his chest is broad enough to serve a meal, four courses and desert. The guy is talking to me and now I get to answer him.

"Yes, I'm new here. I'm just visiting." I scan again for Alita. I don't want to talk to anyone, but also don't want to be rude.

"I've lived here for ten years. I'd love to show you my France. We can eat and love as you see Paris as it is meant to be seen."

"No, thank you." I think back on the last lovers I've had. Major disappointments. Besides, I'm here on some serious business, not to be getting picked up by a bicycle riding, tennis shoe wearing grown ass man.

"I insist. You look ready to be free in the city of love." He steps closer and tries to take my hand.

I fold my arms and tell him, "No, I'm not ready to be free. I mean I'm free. No, no. I mean no."

I try to get away from him. He sticks like cotton on tape.

"Come, come, we can be so much more than friends. We will explore the city. Take my number"

Just as I am ready to scream, Alita is by my side. She quickly sizes up the situation and says to Mr. Speedo, "Hello, are you attempting to entice?" Then she turns to me to say, "Lynn, you have met a new friend. Do you choose to spend some time with him?"

I turn horrified eyes towards her. I can imagine the headline. "Stupid Ass Kansas Woman Picks up Tennis Shoe Wearing Mass Murderer."

"No Alita. I don't want to go anywhere with him, but he won't leave me alone."

He chimes in, "I want to show you Paris."

The funicular stops and we exit, with him still attached to one side and Alita attached at the other.

"I am seeing Paris with my friend. I can't go with you." I look to Alita for some help and she doesn't fail me.

"Thank you for the offer. She may have felt differently if she were to be here longer. Why not give her your number. If she has some free time, she will contact you," Alita says with a smile.

Island man removes pencil and paper from his bicycle bag and writes down his number. "Call me if you please." He pushes the paper towards me and I take it. He gets on his bike and pedals off, looking back once to say, "You call."

"Alita, can you believe that? He tried to pick me up."

She smiles and says, "You meet people, you meet people" then she moves around the area.

We are in the midst of an artistic community Alita tells me is called Montmartre. Right around the bend, there are paintings with every color imaginable. The crowd moves in symphony, in circular motions around stalls. Artists sit in front of their wares, and everything is being sold from small five inch by eight inch scenes, to six foot wide views of the Eiffel Tower and Notre Dame.

Alita and I move through the throng, with her being stopped and hugged along the way. I love the feel of the city. The smiles and greetings are nice, but I still feel a bit isolated from everything around me. English is the only language I am fluent in and the chatter is wearing thin on my nerves since I only understand one word in thirty. I go to stand and look down the mountain at a panoramic view of the city.

My romantic side thinks it would have been nice to see Paris with Robert. To be honest, it might not be as enjoyable a city with Robert trying to own my every thought and action. When I go back home, there is the opportunity to get my old life back. I wouldn't have to sleep alone. I couldn't sleep in the middle of the bed anymore and would have to stay on my side all night so Robert won't be disturbed. Travel would still be solo since Robert does not believe in traveling but there would be someone for me.

Alita is watching me. She gives a small headshake with a smile to make me wonder if she still misses the man we shared. Her life appears full; maybe she has moved on. It's time for me to do the same. At the end of the thought, I'm depressed again.

"Come ma petite, let the sorrowful thoughts go and enjoy Paris."

Three hours pass quickly. I've had my picture taken in front of the Eiffel Tower, seen more monuments than I'll ever remember, and rode a funicular. As we are waiting for Etienne, Alita starts the conversation she had wanted to start when I arrived in Paris.

"Lynn, what is it you are seeking?"

"Oh, there's Etienne."

I wave as if we don't stand out already and Alita could not be seen from five blocks away in her flowing yellow dress. The reality is I don't know how to answer her question. I don't know what I'm looking for. I accepted the divorce, and know I'm single. But what do you do with singleness? Divorced, single again, solo, dumped and with little effort I could add bitter to my list of descriptors. But I could have my old life back.

As Etienne gets us bundled in, Alita smiles at me.

"A delay, but questions must be answered, if only for your own clarity."

Once we get back to her home, I plead a headache and go to my room to rest. A few minutes later there is a knock at the door. Please don't be Alita to pressure me. I don't know my own mind yet, so I can't answer any questions. "Come in."

"May I be of service to you in any way?" Louis is standing tall and is the epitome of maleness with a sensual smile.

"Uh. I have a headache." That can't be a come-on line he's giving me. If it is, the headache plea will dampen his attempt to seduce me, if he is trying to seduce me.

"Would you like some headache powder or perhaps a glass of chardonnay to assist you in resting?"

"A glass of chardonnay would be nice."

"I shall attend to it immediately."

Not five minutes later, Louis is back with a long stemmed glass of white wine and a gleaming silver tray effortlessly held in his left hand. He has an arrangement of cheese, and grapes, and crackers.

He enters and places the serving tray on the side table. When he has everything displayed to his liking, he turns to me.

"If there is any other thing you desire to assist you in resting, please let me know." He gives me a smile and shows all of his pearly whites, executes a head nod, and leaves the room.

No he didn't! No. I'm sure he didn't. That wasn't an invitation. I eat my cheese and grapes while sipping wine and considering Louis's comments and Alita's question.

What am I looking for? I'm looking for me. The me that was lost thirty years ago when my dreams extended beyond being a mother and a wife. Dreams that challenged me to be fearless and see the world. That's why it's so tempting to return to what is safe and known, my role as Robert's wife. I don't know how to do anything else.

With those thoughts spinning in my head, it starts to hurt in earnest. Now is a great time to rest and sleep comes easily. My dream starts wonderfully. I'm climbing the Eiffel Tower. With each step closer to the top, I'm growing larger and larger. The air seems to make my lungs expand enough for me to smell the earth and breathe the freshness of the heat from the sun in the sky. I feel strong enough to walk back to Wichita, crossing the ocean with two steps.

Just when I'm ready to step to the top rung of the Tower, there is someone pulling at my ankle. I look down and it's Robert. He's yelling at me to come back down because the children are getting frightened. I see my daughters crying and begging me to come back. Robert pulls me back down, one rung at a time, fussing every step of the way. With each step my body shrinks until it returns to my normal size returns. I had almost made it to the top but allowed him to pull me back to the ground. My eyes return and stay glued to the point at the top of the monument as we walk away. Robert doesn't give me a chance to speak; rather he continues to chastise.

"Lynn, what do you think you were doing? That was totally stupid. You've upset the children. You could have fallen."

"But Robert did you see me? I wasn't falling; I almost made it to the top."

"For what? There's nothing for you to do at the top but fall. Now come on. It's time to go home. It's Monday and you have to fix our stew so we can be in bed before ten."

The thought of cutting beef for stew, my least favorite food, brings me out of sleep. But the three hours of walking around Paris keep me in bed. I doze back to sleep.

I flow into the next dream where I am in the dining room with Alita having lunch with Maya Angelou. We are chattering away like old friends, discussing their amazing journeys through life.

Maya asks me "Lynn what do you plan to do with your time here on earth? How will you make your mark?"

"I thought I would start with…"

Suddenly there is a commotion in the hallway. Robert is coming in with a pair of handcuffs and a blindfold.

"Lynn, it's time to come home. Get your things."

"Robert I was having lunch with Alita and Maya Angelou. Let me introduce you to them."

"I don't need to meet them. Come on, I've come to take you home where you belong."

"What if I don't belong there anymore?"

"Don't be foolish. Of course you belong at home. Come on."

I see Alita, Etienne, and Louis watching from various parts of the room Maya Angelou continues to eat and watches me.

"What shall you do Lynn? Will you go gladly back to your cage to sing?" Maya asks as she dips her spoon into her soup and brings it to her lips.

The others watch as though frozen. Alita's eyes reflect the same question Maya verbalized.

"What should I do?" My question is to the entire room, but no one answers at first.

"Come home," Robert is calling to me.

"Remove your stress so you can decide," Maya says.

"Follow your heart," says Alita.

I am about to tell them all what I will do when I wake up, unsettled and confused. The idea of getting up doesn't appeal to me and I drift back to sleep. An hour later I wake up not one bit refreshed. Those must have been chardonnay induced dreams. There is a quiet tapping on the door and it opens to admit Alita.

"Have you finished hiding?"

"I wasn't hiding, I was experiencing jet lag." Her look suggests she doesn't quite believe me.

"Are you ready to talk?"

"Yes, I guess so."

"So what made you decide to come for the false burial?"

"I didn't have anything better to do and I want some adventure."

"Adventure? Lynn, what do you really want from life? You're a world away from home, did you come for the adventure?"

"I'm trying to find some purpose for me. Since the divorce, I've been existing, marking time. When your offer came, it seemed perfect. More than anything else, it gave me an opportunity to get away. As far away from Robert and his new love, the pity of my children, the disappointment I think my father feels, as possible."

"So the divorce was not your idea?"

"No. it came as a shock to find out my husband was cheating, and an even bigger shock to find he no longer wanted me. But just before I left, he told me he wants us to get back together."

"And do you want to get back together?"

"I don't know. I could have it all back. The opportunity to be secure and safe is tempting."

"What are his thoughts about the time you shared with our husband?"

"I never told him about it.

"Yet you are thinking of reconciling with him. Will you tell him then?"

"No."

"Why."

"I couldn't explain the why to him; he would never understand what it was because I can't understand it myself. And unless you are coming to Wichita, he won't be hearing about it."

We both laugh and think about the events in Nashville.

"So you have been celibate."

'Not exactly. I've kissed some frogs and did some travelling at home thanks to your husband."

"And were you satisfied."

"No I was more bored than anything else. I learned sometimes, it's not worth taking your clothes off. Heck I couldn't even get self gratification right. And now I must admit I've been feeling rather twitchy." I shake my head and fall silent remembering my disastrous sexual exploits.

"Twitchy? What is twitchy?"

"You know." I wave my hand around the lower part of my body and give head nods. "Twiiiitttchy"

Alita makes sympathetic sounds and says, "Oh. Twitchy. So what is it you are seeking? A great romance?"

"Happily ever after does not exist. I don't really want to be at Robert's beck and call. I want a man that would allow and encourage me to be me. Maybe I'm looking for me, to fulfill my dreams that challenged me to be fearless and see the world."

"So easy to accomplish. Why not start with Europe. See some of the sites here. You could have some adventures while you are in this part of the world. Perhaps you should visit some different countries after we return from the false burial. Then you can go back to Wichita and make the decisions for your life."

"How can I do that?"

"Almost everywhere is accessible by train. We also have local airlines that take you from here to anywhere."

I start fidgeting with the coverlet on the bed. Thoughts are tumbling over in my head while my mind attempts to sort and plan my words. "What if I get lost?"

"Ma petit, you are already lost. Find yourself. There are no deadlines, no hurry. Take your time, embrace life. Embrace your choices."

"I can't go alone. Will you come with me?"

"No, this is a journey you must undertake alone."

"I don't know. This was a pretty big step. I would be gone too long if I went anywhere else."

"This experience may help you. It appears you have been pampered almost your whole life, with decisions made for you. Now it is time for you to spread your wings. You must make this decision and the decision you make will make you. There is much to see out there if only you would open your eyes."

"What if something happens?'

"Something like what?"

"I don't know. Anything."

"What if nothing happens? What is something wonderful happens? What would failure look like?"

"I don't know"

"What would success look like?"

"I don't know?"

"What would you need to decide these things?"

"I would need to feel like I'm ready for anything. What if I meet someone? I don't think I'm ready. Remember San Antonio, Phoenix and Vancouver?"

"You know how to plan. He often spoke of your tourist activities."

"He talked about me?"

"Certainly. We talked about everything."

"I don't even think I'm clear on what I would want in a physical or any other relationship."

"We shall go to Monaco, to a little place I have there."

"What kind of place?"

"A place for the sensual. Now come, it is time for us to eat. And tomorrow, Brian and Patience will dine with us."

In a whirl of pink silk and lace, she is gone. I don't know if I'm up to her idea of sensual, but what an adventure this will be. I had meant to ask her about Louis and his offer of assistance.

We sit down and have a quiet dinner and discussion about life in general and travel in particular.

"Alita, did you ever travel with him when he went to play?"

"In the early days, but then I developed my own interests. If there was time for us to be together while he was on the road, we took advantage of those times. It was not necessary for us to be together physically. Being apart made our time together more sacred."

"I wonder if my relationship with Robert could grow into something as beautiful."

"How long were the two of you married?"

"Over thirty years."

"My people have a saying. If you leave a bucket outside on a rainy day and it does not fill with water from the rain, if you leave it out overnight the dew will not fill it with water either. You have been trying to fill you bucket with your marriage of almost thirty years. Do you honestly think completeness will come now?"

The rest of our meal is completed in silence.

DINNER AND CONVERSATION

The next day we decide to relax around the house. In the afternoon, Alita shows me around her yard and garden. She grows most of the vegetables we have been eating, as well as the herb iced tea we drink.

"Would you like to gather the flowers for the table, Lynn?"

"What do I have to do?"

"Take the basket and put the flowers in that make you smile. Those are the ones that would like to show off. Then you can arrange them for the table."

Alita gives me a basket with a pair of shears and points me towards her flower garden. It must be designed to match her clothing. The same vibrant shades are growing in no particular order.

Gather the flowers that make me smile. I can try. The blue flowers growing like trumpets make me smile. As do the yellow ones with the brown center. A red velvety flower makes me not only smile but run it over my face after I cut it. Once I think I have enough to make a decent centerpiece, I head indoors swinging my basket and savoring the simplicity, the living in the beauty of the moment.

Brian and Patience arrive and we sit in the living room having a glass of wine and chatting. Brian starts talking about his passion, music.

"Lynn, please understand Brian disdains music that is not jazz. He likes the purity," Patience tells me.

"Not true not true," Brian laughs. "Nobody can crack a note better than Tina Turner." He tells us.

We enter into a spirited conversation about Miles Davis, Herbie Hancock and rap music. Louis enters the room with three men I recognize. One by one, Shaun, Leon and Willie come over to hug me.

Shaun says, "Imagine meeting you here. I always ask what happened to you."

Leon says, "Time passes quickly. It is good to see you again."

Willie comes forward to tell me, "Well met."

"Dear ones, it is so good of you to come. You remember Brian and Patience."

After much hugging and back slapping, we return to our conversation. We talk about more jazz and male greats from W. C. Handy to Wynton Marsalis. Finally we agree that Aretha is indeed the queen after Alita puts on the Live in Paris recording from the 60's.

As we turn to other aspects of the male side of the music equation, Brian shows off more of his knowledge as he talks about James Brown's impact on music. We make our way into the dining room for our meal. My fantastic centerpiece graces the table and makes me smile.

Brian talks about beats and hitting on the one. We are all participating, sharing thoughts and ideas and I am an equal part of the conversation in a way I never was allowed to talk with Robert present. Patience is an active part of the conversation and not a rubber stamp of Brian's ideas.

I remember early in my marriage when Robert and I still interacted with others. I disagreed on who was the best actor of all time. When we got home, he lectured me on the importance of having a united front when we are around others. That united front became critical in private conversation also. Then the united front became only his point of view he expected me to share and make my own.

"What is the one?" I ask being the only non-musician.

"The first note out of the instrument. James made people focus on the very first note, not wait until the third or fourth," Brian explains. He took the canvas and changed things.

"I don't get it," I admit although it is clear everyone else does.

Shaun says, "Think of music as a blank canvas with musicians as the artist. As the drummer, I start the work of art. I give the constant, the lines, bold lines for loud notes, narrow lines for the softer ones. I keep everyone in time. That's my job, to create the parameter for everyone to work within, make the opening for everyone else to contribute. I initialize the painting, draws lines, straight, bold, thick or narrow."

Willie chimes in, "As the pianist, I make the curved lines. I take the solids Shaun puts out and make circles and wave lines, cross what he has out there, bend them and then the listener can follow the melody."

"Guitars and horns connect the lines giving symmetry and balance. They weave between lines filling in the blank spaces, adding shape. I give the definition," Leon shares.

I ask, "So what did he do for the music?"

Alita answers, "Percussion adds emphasis, tells you where to look and when, brings out the intensity of the eyes, the strength of the tree bark, the height of the wave."

"When we play together, the picture gets color. When we play from our soul, our audience can see our picture in the full spectrum of color," Shaun contributes. "They can close their eyes to see the color of happiness and sorrow. Without words, there appears the tangible color of love, loss and hope. When we color the music right, our audience becomes a living part of our picture."

"And that is where the hitting comes in. Do you place the emphasis on the first note or the third? Is it a bold stroke or not. Maybe the second note is the hook or the last is what you want people to gravitate towards."

The conversation eventually heads towards the museum exhibit. Patience broaches the subject. "I understand you didn't like the exhibit at the museum.

"No I didn't care for the exhibit. I thought it was very racist. What did you think Patience?"

"Being African American, I understand completely how you feel."

Brian pipes up, "I think the problem is they had so much material and no idea what it was or the significance of the depictions. The curator did not do a good job with the amazing amount of memorabilia in his possession."

"Some of it should not have been shown."

"But then we would have missed out on the thoughts of the musicians," Patience puts out.

They all join in and describe the music with a series of noises to imitate the instruments. Their passion is clearly in the music. As they talk and I interject, Alita picks up a pad from the table and begins moving her hand quickly and determinedly across the paper.

I pull back and watch my dinner companions. They are all leading full lives, doing what they love to do, and allowing me to be a part of their conversation, helping me to understand and to see music through the eyes of the musician. That gets me thinking about my life, or rather what my life could be if I decide to return to my life with Robert. Yes I could have my life back, but at what cost.

I jump back into the conversation to avoid the thoughts. At the end of the evening, everyone is sated by the food, wine and conversation. Alita passes around the paper she had been preoccupied with after dinner.

Patience is the first to comment. "Alita, once again, you have captured the essence of the evening. No wonder your work is so sought after."

When it finally gets to my hands, I have to agree with Patience. It is a rendering of us at the table, all talking and gesturing energetically. Everyone comments on how lifelike the scene is and how well Alita captured the features and the feelings of everyone present.

"I will make several and send one to all of you." Alita retrieves the drawing and puts it on a side table.

Brian and Patience stand. Patience tells the room at large, "We've got to run. We will be going home in a few days. Alita it's always a pleasure. Lynn, here's our number. Give us a call when you get back to the States."

"It was a pleasure meeting you, Patience and seeing you again, Brian. I had a wonderful time." I turn to the fellows and get a hug from each of them.

Willie asks, "Lynn, why did you never come to see us again? He always left a ticket for you. We always thought we would see you when we were touring."

"Why didn't I come? I guess because I hate goodbyes." I hug each of them and try not to regret the decisions I made.

Finally, everyone is gone. The lost opportunities are on my mind when I hear Alita's voice.

"Ma petite, the past is gone. Look forward." She comes over to give me a comforting hug. "It is late, I must rest now."

Look forward, there's a scary thought. I go and send an e-mail home to Lynnette.

Hello,

Just wanted to let you know I saw the sights in Paris and will be heading to Cannes and Monaco tomorrow. I rode a funicular and didn't fall off.

Give everyone my love. Having a wonderful time.

Peace, Love and Music

Your Mother

Thoughts of the future plague me as I go to my bedroom. Hopefully my night dreams will not be a repetition of the afternoon nap time. I don't want to dream about Robert tonight.

MAN OH MONACO

The next morning, Alita tells me to pack enough for two nights. I throw some things in my overnighter and consider myself prepared. We take a small plane to Nice then the train to Cannes before arriving midday.

Alita has everything in order and the trip is smooth. We go to a restaurant on the beach at Cannes. Waiters greet Alita with a kiss on each cheek. After the fourth greeting I give in to my curiosity.

"Do you come here often? You seem to know everyone."

"You meet people, because you meet people."

The intrigue and mystery surrounding her only increases as a tall man in a black suit walks quickly our way.

"You have come." He reaches out to embrace Alita.

She quickly moves one arm across her face and the other across her chest preventing his touch. Etienne steps between the two of them.

"Never are you permitted to touch me." She stares at him for a second before turning her head and walking away.

I follow, puzzled by the exchange. We sit down and peruse the menu, which is thankfully in French and English, as I wait for her to talk about what just happened. This is the first time I had ever seen anything ruffle her composure.

Whoever the guy is, he's still on the other side of the restaurant staring at her like a lost puppy. She is back to her composed untroubled self. If she sees him over there, she gives no indication. A short while later two waiters approach him and walk with him to the door. I want some background and fill in on what the hell is going on. I am a guest so I guess it is none of my damn business.

Alita looks up and says, "Are you ready to order?"

"Sure, what do you recommend?"

"Whatever appeals to you."

She looks up and our waiter arrives with a plate. Four little pieces of bread with black spots of something peeking out from a white cream sauce are accompanied by a three fingers high glass filled with white liquid.

Alita takes a bit of the bread and tosses the liquid in her mouth in one gulp. She smiles and gestures for me to try.

I didn't come this far to be a wimp about food. It looks like it's a cold soup and the little black things are mushrooms. French people eat strange looking food, but I'm game. When in Cannes, do all you can.

I bite the bread and it is perfection. It has a nice crust with an airy light inside and a slight taste of herbs. Picking up the glass, my throat is expecting a smile. I toss it back like Alita did. When the concoction hits the back of my throat, tears cloud my eyes. The only taste is salt, the main ingredient. Bits and pieces of something that may have been alive are going down my throat quickly followed by a desire to sandpaper the taste off of my tongue.

Alita looks at me and smiles. "There is no shame in rejecting what is offered. Everything is not good and you may reject what is not pleasing."

She could have told me it tasted like shit before I put it in my mouth.

"Well if I had known it would taste so bad, I wouldn't have tried it."

"But you would not have known the flavor. After tasting, you know what you do not like. Sometimes it is worth trying and sometimes you reject based on past experience."

"Is that the rule you live by?"

"The man you saw approach me, when our husband died, he wanted to claim me. His offer to me would tempt others to accept, if they are focused on the material things. Material things are not what appeal to me. I have what I desire materially and can accept nothing less than a man who is secure enough to allow me to be who I am, without feeling threatened. Claude wants me so he can change me, to make me what I am not. That is not acceptable to me, so he no longer has access to my life."

"Do you think you will ever marry again?"

"Only if I can find such a one, secure enough to allow me to exist in my fullness. Only on my terms as I find I cannot settle for less than what I have had before."

I think about her words and marvel at her strength. Only on her terms, how powerful an approach to life.

The waiter soon returns to take our order. Thankful for the translations beside each dish, I select the salmon in dill sauce along with white wine. Alita has the king prawns with a cream sauce.

"Tell me about Liberian culture, what should I expect to see?"

"Lynn what do you want to know about?"

"Well the wife thing has me a little confused."

"Why? Because men can have multiple wives?"

"Yes, how does it work?"

"Generally the first wife is chosen by the mother of the husband. She is looking for someone able to run a home and raise the children. The second wife is chosen by the first wife. The first wife is looking for someone to help with wifely duties. She must be able to get along with the second wife for the sake of harmony. The husband chooses the third and any subsequent wives. The first two wives have veto power and they are all considered mates although the first wife is always the head wife."

Her conversation takes us through dinner. Soon after we finish, Etienne appears.

"Shall we go, Lynn?"

Etienne takes us to the train station and we take a short ride to Monaco. Once we arrive Alita leads the way to the outside curb.

"We will wait here for the car."

She steps forward and a car quickly pulls up. Alita motions me to get into the back of a sleek black Mercedes. The driver is a stranger. He is handsome, with a salt and pepper beard and the body of a football player. His broad shoulders strain against the confines of his jacket. His mouth turns to show a glimpse of his teeth between his soft juicy lips when he smiles at me and says, "Bon jour."

"Where's Etienne?"

"Etienne is France" she replies before performing the introduction. "Lynn, this is Enufu. He will be our aide in Monaco."

"Oh. Do you have aides all over?

"Pretty much. It makes life interesting."

We start the drive up into the mountains. At the hotel lobby, Alita turns to ask, "Are you prepared to embrace the sensual?"

Sensual and I have not had extensive interactions. My time with her husband was the closest I have been to sensual. Dreams of him still have me waking up on the verge of an orgasm.

"Yes. I'm as prepared as I'll ever get.?"

Alita smiles, her lips turning up and her eyes conveying excitement. She leads the way to the elevator and puts a key into a partially hidden slot at the top row of numbers before pressing an unnumbered button. Seconds later, the doors open.

This reminds me of what it would be like to be stepping into the twilight zone. Instead we are in a large room with a view of the ocean coming through the far wall made entirely of glass. French doors lead to a balcony. To the left are closed doors. The wall on the right is mirrored from the floor to the ceiling. A large bed occupies the space on a dais in the center of the room.

Directly over the bed, mirrors magnify the pillows of various shapes, sizes and textures. The bed is easily ten feet long and sits three feet off the floor. A small step stool is at the side. All around the bed are glass three foot pedestals with candles.

Enufu takes my luggage through one of the closed doors on the left. A short time later, Enufu takes me through a door into a spacious bedroom with my clothes hanging in the closet and folded neatly in the chest of drawers in the corner. The bed is beautifully made with a pink hand crocheted throw in various shades of purples and reds. It looks fluffy enough to be a pillow.

"You may rest in private or in public, which would you prefer?"

There is a totally decadent bed and the door Enufu and I just came back through. "I'll rest later."

"Would you like to see Monaco?"

"Don't mind if I do."

We get back into the car and take a ride around the small country. We follow the route of the Grand Prix race and go to the extensive aquarium. Enufu is knowledgeable about every corner of the country and his sense of humor makes every space exciting.

We get something to eat and go back to the hotel. Alita takes my hand and leads me to the bed.

"Rest ma petite, you will need your energy for tomorrow."

Her words send a shudder through me. I don't know if it is from apprehension or anticipation. The bed, once I climb in, feels like a cloud of bubbles. Curling up, it is easy for me to relax and then allow my eyes to drift up at the mirror on the ceiling. "It's funny how little this bed makes me look, Alita."

"That is only because you are currently alone here."

I drift off to sleep to with the sound of Alita's laughter in my ears.

It seems only a few minutes pass before Alita wakes me up. "It is time to wake and shower. Here is something easy to wear."

It is late morning and we go down to the hotel restaurant for brunch. When we're finished eating, we go back to the room. I go out on the balcony and spend time thinking until Alita comes out with Enufu in tow and asks, "Are you ready to experience pleasure?"

"Probably. What happens next?"

Alita gives me a soft frothy creation similar to the yellow peignoir she is holding, only pink. Two lace ribbons are used to close the transparent fabric at the breast and the crotch. It does little to keep out the air.

Enufu leads me to the bathroom. The walk-in shower has water spraying from all sides. The warm water does nothing to stop the goose bumps. When I step out of the shower, Enufu is there with a large blue towel to help me dry off and lead me back to the bed.

"Enufu and I will help you to decide what you like. Once you know what you like, you will seek that, or continue to experiment"

"Okay, Alita."

"Preparation is the key to pleasure. Put the thought into what you are feeling," Alita tells me.

"Please lie down, face down," he tells me.

Enufu takes my right foot, Alita my left.

"Leave nothing out, take nothing for granted," Enufu cautions.

His strong fingers take my right foot in his hand. He grasps a toe and rotates it, kneads it, and repeats the process on the sole of my foot.

Alita is copying his movements. Although her touch is firm, it is a far cry from the deep penetration of Enufu's fingers. She rotates my foot and speaks.

"Watching hands move over you allow your senses to expand."

They are kneading the calf of my leg. Then they touch the back of my knee and working up to my thighs. I am watching them from the strategically placed mirror Enufu had placed on the floor so I can see the reflection in the overhead mirrors.

The twin hands spend time on my ass, squeezing spreading. My lungs forget to expand. My eyes are glued to the sight of four hands on my ass and working upward.

Their fingers alternately intertwine as each finds a niche in my spine. They manipulate, allowing an ease of tension, all the more profound because I wasn't aware of being tense. Enufu's fingers on the side of my ribs delineate each one and combine with his deep rich voice.

"Your body will tell you how to touch, what to touch,"

My shoulders enjoy the ministrations from the two of them.

"Time to turn" Alita tells me.

A view of myself in the mirror overhead causes the blood to flow to my face.

"This didn't look so decadent from behind."

Enufu and Alita return to the bottom of my body. They quickly come to the place my body wants touched most. Alita looks at me and smiles. This is old territory for her since she touched me before giving me to her husband. She runs her fingers through my pubic hair. Enufu's fingers copy her movements.

"The dichotomy of the hard and soft increases the intensity of feeling" Alita tell me as she slips a soft finger inside of me.

"Which do you prefer?" Enufu is watching me intently as his larger harder finger enters the same hole. My eyes drift closed as the orgasm continues to build.

"Open your eyes," Alita and Enufu tell me in unison.

I comply and see both of them watching me. My eyes travel to the mirror and watch their fingers entering and exiting a very wet me. My hips start to move.

The soft feathery touch of Alita has me moving closer to her tender fingers. But Enufu's strength, the feel of the callous pads on his fingers, has me moving closer towards him. I look in the mirror and my hips resemble a large ping pong ball going side to side.

"Tell me what you see," Alita purrs.

"I see myself wide open, I see your fingers moving in and out of me, hard, soft, fast, deep." My eyes open wider and my hips start to move faster. "I see me ready to come." My mouth opens on a scream of ecstasy I'm surprised didn't break the glass in the windows.

Enufu and Alita withdraw their fingers and lean over me to kiss each other. Then each brings a hand to cover my brand new breasts. The new nipples are rock hard.

Alita looks at me and smiles. "How do you feel?"

"On edge, waiting, wanting something, but not sure what the wait is for. I'm also a bit confused. This is the second time you've seen me naked and had your hands all over me. I don't know how I feel about that."

Alita comes to sit on the bed. Enufu leaves the room. "What is your concern?"

"It's hard to put into words. I mean, you did some really intense things." My voice drops to a whisper, "You went all up in me."

"And?"

I see I have to get more specific with her. "Well, that can't be right."

Alita asks, "Why is there a right?"

"Because there has to be. I mean if you don't know right, you don't know wrong." That sounds crazy as hell and I'm the one that said it.

"Maybe you are too focused on right or wrong. Maybe, you should just feel for a while. Get to know yourself, what you like and don't like. There is no harm in refusing what you dislike and accepting what you do. Free yourself and embrace passion, Lynn."

"Free myself. What a tantalizing thought, Alita."

"There is a gathering tonight. Would you like to come or stay in the room and your comfort zone?"

The thought is tempting enough for me to ask, "What will they do there? I don't want to get in the middle of an orgy."

"You would need to come and see. Decide if you want an adventure or solitude. You are free to experience pleasure or not. You may join or watch. You can be free and you can chose."

Stay safe or go adventuring. Given I'm in Monaco and had my first sexual encounter in a group setting, the answer is easy. "I'm game. What should I wear?"

"That depends on if you want to be easily accessible or not."

"My standard black dress should do the trick. What will we do until then?"

"Take your time. The show will not start until we arrive. Why not go out and see Nice. There is good food there. They have the best socca anywhere."

"By myself?"

"Sure. English is freely spoken and you can travel by train. Enufu will go with you."

"Sure why not." I gather some money and Enufu to go out adventuring. "Nice it is. We'll be back before it gets dark."

Enufu points out items of interest as we catch the train into Nice. He also knows the best stores and takes me around the city to shoe shops, clothing stores and a quiet restaurant at the end of a curving street that narrows into a pathway.

"Here we can have socca." He orders what looks like a large crepe. It is a light airy type of bread with a hummus paste in the middle. We wash it down with a chilled white wine and people watch until the sun starts roasting us then head back. Alita is out of sight and I decide to get a quick shower.

It takes a while to freshen up and get ready for an evening of something new. I think about the experience of male and female, soft and hard and need to wash certain parts again. I pull out my little red corset and the matching stockings. A look in the mirror and the reflection shows my breasts filling the cups like the foam coming over a cup of chocolate latte. When the dress settles around my hips, I feel sexy.

Back in the outer room, Alita and Enufu are already there. She has on a pink flowing cloud of fabric that shimmers and shakes with each breath she takes. It ties on the side with a large purple ribbon.

Enufu looks damn fine in a silk shower wrap and probably nothing else. He comes toward me and says, "You look ravishing."

We head out of the door and into the glass elevator made into the side of the mountain. We exit on a floor with a glass wall allowing a floor to ceiling view of the ocean. The mountain is on the opposite wall. We head into a large ballroom.

"Look," Enufu whispers as he points upward.

A large glass elevator located in the center of the room starts its descent. It is decorated with white lights and gold paint, rather like a moving chandelier. As it slowly gets lower, the participants inside, two men and one woman become more visible. The crowd gathers around and watches from below as the elevator inhabitants start to disrobe.

The first man is well over six feet and black as the inside of a cave at midnight. His torso glistens as he reveals a body that has been built to muscular perfection. His arms could crush stone and I imagine how it would feel to be held by that much strength. I don't want to take my eyes off of him. But I have to look at the other elevator occupants.

The next male is significantly shorter and as they continue to undress, it is apparent he is noticeably smaller in the area where size matters. He has a black leather harness around his broad chest area. The harness comes down to split his ass and up the front to allow his maleness to release through a small hole before ending in a large gold buckle that connects the harness fit right above his navel.

His ass cheeks resemble two perfectly baked cupcakes, fresh from the oven with a glistening sheen. He wears his blond hair in a ponytail that falls between his shoulder blades to the middle of his back. It is held in place with a leather string and he has six inch leather cuffs with gold studs around his wrists and lower legs. His smooth body is a stark contrast to Mr. Manly who sports hair on his chest but has shaved all of the hair off of his head.

My hands go to cover my eyes, but my fingers allow me to peek through and see what is happening.

"Open your eyes and watch the feast," Alita tells me.

The lone woman has disrobed. Her generous breasts are now swaying with the movement of the elevator, which is coming down uncommonly slowly. As it nears our heads, the elevator stops.

"Oh my damn," says a woman wearing three strands of pearls. She is fingering her pearls with one hand and fanning herself with the other hand. It does nothing to alleviate the sweat breaking out on her upper lip and forehead. Her light colored dress shows the moisture from her neck, chest and underarms and pelvic area.

The woman in the elevator drops to her knees to accept the enlarged shaft of the first male participant. He is putting ten to eleven inches, by my estimation, somewhere in her throat unless she has a hole in the back of her head we aren't able to see. He is moving in slow motion and so is she. The assembled group of thirty people starts applauding.

Mr. Blond ponytail bends down behind the woman in the man sandwich and spreads her legs wide enough for us to see what she had for breakfast. But he doesn't stop there. He lifts her by her hips while bringing her to his mouth and eats her from the middle. It's like she is a cookie and he's getting the cream filling. All the while she keeps her mouth around Mr. Manly's dick.

As the elevator finally comes completely to the bottom of the floor, the audience gives applause as the doors open. The large recipient of what has to be the world's most erotic blow job exits and takes a bow. He reaches back to give a hand to the body of the mouth that can open wide as a balloon.

The very limber lady without a gag reflex exits. She smiles and waves before discreetly and coyly wiping the corner of her mouth. Her bow sets her ample breasts swinging before she places her hands inadequately over the nipples. She turns and reaches back to bring out the last participant.

The man with the voracious appetite and tremendous upper body strength comes out. His long hair is no longer contained by his leather string and is moving freely around his shoulders. He lifts up both arms and makes his pecs dance. He has his chest muscles go up and down in and out and if you get hit with one, it would knock you out.

Again the audience applauds. The first two drift off to mingle with the crowd. The blond drops to all fours as he is approached by a tall toffee colored woman wearing a leather hat tilted to the left with attitude.

Her leather earrings, the single leather cuff on her arm, and the studs on her leather boots match the designs on the blond man. She brings out a gold leash that ends with a leather holder. She moves his hair and attaches the leash to the harness on his neck.

Once he is secured, he comes around and buries his face between her legs. She strokes his hair and murmurs what a good pet he is and how proud she is of his performance. He keeps his nose buried in her personal space.

What the hell. Alita is ever the social butterfly and starts flitting from grouping to grouping. I feel like a wide-eyed puppy in a pet store, wanting to look at everyone that comes in to see what will happen next. Now the show is over, conversation is again flowing.

"Close your mouth or someone may mistake it for an invitation," Alita whispers in my ear.

My mouth snaps shut. "Alita, does everything go on here?"

"Nothing goes on without the approval of everyone participating. Maybe it would be a good idea to walk around and see what there is to see, think about what you would like to try, if anything. Here is the room key if you decide to go back there," she sings out as she heads toward the hallway marked Bondage with Enufu.

My head spins at the variety of things to do. To say I feel out of place is so obvious it would be hard to imagine a more unlikely place for me to be standing. The room is large and people are walking around, pairing and grouping, then disappearing through various doors. There are more signs along the wall. Voyeur, Anal, Oral, Male/Male, Female/Female, Group. The voyeur arrow is closest. It must be a sign.

The hallway has windows similar to how newborns are laid out for sightings by families. Most are without the bright lights. The rooms are low lit, but there is a light switch on the outside so you can increase the interior light. Each window gives a description, rather like a name placard. Single, couple, multiple. There is an intercom system so you can speak to the person in the window.

Inside a one window is a woman in a nightgown of sheer red lace. She is wearing heavy makeup and black lace stockings, held up with red garters. Her red heels are at least six inches. They match the red of her lipstick and her nails. The contrast of red on her chocolate brown skin is arresting.

Around her there is an assortment of toys similar to the ones at the adult toy store in Wichita. She also has a set of silver balls like the ones that had gotten stuck in my interior. She parts her lace nightgown and shows off her nicely rounded breasts before walking over to the table beside the bed.

She picks up the balls and caresses them before putting them back down. Damn, I wanted to know what to do with those balls since I couldn't figure out how to work them on my own. This may be my only opportunity to be educated. I press the intercom and hope she speaks English.

"Excuse me Lady in there, could you tell me what you do with those balls? I have some and they weren't very useful."

She stops and looks at me as if she does not get many requests for conversation. She smiles and walks over to the window. "These are called Ben Wa balls. They can be used two ways. They are a perfect way to strengthen your vaginal muscles."

"How?"

"You start with using one. You put it in like this."

She goes back to the bed and puts her right foot on the edge. She holds up a ball to me and then pushes it into herself. My information person comes back to the window to tell me, "You hold it inside. The weight of the ball causes it to come down. The muscles in your vagina are used to keep the ball inside. You start inserting it for an hour or so three times a day and work your way up to being able to keep it in it all day."

"I had a bit of a problem getting the balls out." The idea of going through life, with what I now know are Ben Wa balls, once had me in tears.

My new mentor says, "If you stand and relax, they will come back out. "

"What else can you do with them?"

"You use them with a vibrator. The vibration stimulates them and gives a pleasurable sensation."

She walks back to the bed and lies down, parting her legs and pulling up her nightgown. A man appears at my elbow and watches her through the window. She inserts the second ball. The etiquette for what to say in this situation escapes me. I watch him for a few seconds out of the corner of my eyes before returning my attention back to the window.

The ball in her hand has disappeared. She is lying back onto her bed with a long instrument that vibrates and looks like a penis with a toothbrush at the top. It is vibrating and she is gyrating. The man beside me starts rubbing himself. He finally pulls his dick out and starts stroking. When he finishes what he has started, I am thankful he didn't get any stray droplets on me. He reaches up onto a shelf above the window and pulls out a cloth to clean himself up before sauntering off.

I look at the woman in the window. "Can you see out here?"

'Yes, there is a monitor above the window to show me what is going on. I find it entertaining to be the catalyst, if you will pardon the expression, for so much activity." She stops her play and sits up.

"Is this your favorite spot then?"

"No, it's not. I rather like the conversation spot," she shares with me.

"What do you do there?"

"I give voice to the fantasy. Eroticism is about more than touching bodies." She comes back over to the window.

"You mean like talking sexy?"

"It's a bit more than just talking, sexy. It is creating the scene, using words to build an expectation, to build desire."

I think about her words for a moment. "I bet I could do a conversation."

"Try it, there is nothing to lose. Just remember to visualize the scene and then describe it to your lover. You'll enjoy it and so will your partner."

"Thanks, I'll keep that in mind. It was nice talking to you and I appreciate the information." I wander around and look in a window at a trio. It takes too much effort to separate whose arms belong to who so I walk further. The Bondage people look interesting. The idea of wearing leather unleashes something primitive. I watch and get heated when the Mistress has her naked man sit and follow her around a dining room. She has total control and I've never considered myself a control freak. Until now.

Further ahead is the sign for Auditory. It may be interesting since my exhibitionist likes it. The couple in the window are completely dressed and are sitting with their backs to each other separated by a screen so there is only the ability for them to hear. I don't know what they were saying before, but I get to the speaker in the hallway to hear her question to him.

"No? Then you have thought about what position would we be in?"

"Position?"

"What position would we be in when we do this for the first time? I'm sure you've thought about it. I've seen you looking at my ass and my other assets. I think you would want to come from behind me. Am I right?"

"Yes." The word comes from deep down in his throat and is tortured as a fish being pulled from water.

"Why that position?" she asks as she starts fondling her breasts through her very sheer blouse.

"Because I would dominate you. I would put my hands on your hips and your body would respond to whatever direction I tilt it towards. I would see your spine, the core of your life. And I would be at the end of that line, moving you in the direction I want. Going as deep as I want, making you accept all of me or as little as I choose to give." He looks like he wouldn't be giving her much beyond the conversation. I can see why this is the area he chose.

"Well that could be nice. I could probably take all of you, if I wanted to, only if I wanted you in me that deep."

Even though the conversation is a turn-on, I have to resist the urge to tap on the glass and tell her not to waste her time with him. He's probably got three inches by the quarter sized lump in his pants.

She tells him, "But then, think what I would do to you."

"What do you mean?" his voice comes out as a whisper.

"An even exchange is no robbery."

"What would you do?"

"I would give you a reason to call my name when we are together and to scream my name when you wake up in the middle of the night remembering."

"I doubt it, I'd make love to you all night," he says.

This is ridiculous. He's lying to her about his equipment and I think she would be sadly disappointed. A tall bald gentleman comes to the window and listens for awhile before saying. "I'm Carlos, I noticed you watching. Would you care to play for the night?"

"Play?"

"Yes. I'd like for us to spend the night together."

His words are casual enough to be offering me a piece of gum. He stands around six three, and he is broad enough to lie down on. He is bald and his head has a five o'clock shadow. He has a mustache and goatee with hands big enough to span my thigh.

I start to head back to the main room, a little nervous and a little excited.

"May I walk with you," he asks as he falls in step beside me.

"If you like. I came with some people and need to speak with them." I don't want to go spending the night with someone. He could be a known pervert. Alita and Enufu are milling about.

She sees us and comes over to say, "Do you wish to retire?"

"Not yet. Could I talk to you for a minute? Excuse me Carlos."

We walk away from the gentlemen far enough for me to question her.

"Alita, this guy wants to spend the night. The problem is I've had some horrible sexual experiences lately. Maybe I shouldn't."

"These horrible experiences, were they worth the undressing?"

I think back on the men I had met. "One was about as substantial as a teensy fly and I don't care what people say about size, it matters. The other was finished before I started, and the third almost drowned me."

"But was it worth it?"

"It was worth it because I refused to let them use me. I found the strength to wake them up and be okay with sleeping alone. It sounds weird, but I did learn something."

"Now you must decide if this man is worth it, worth the undressing."

I look over at Carlos.

"Yes. No. Maybe he's not."

"You have to make the decision. Adventures are meant to be interesting. You have the key. We will not be back to the room tonight."

We go back to where Enufu and Carlos are talking.

"Carlos, thank you very much for the offer, but I'll pass. I'd like to look around some more,"

"If that is your choice. Would you care to go to the sensory area?"

"What's in the sensory area?"

"Allow me to show you." He takes my hand and kisses it before tucking it into the crook of his arm and walking us back the way we had come. We enter a darkened hallway where various sex sounds can be heard. There is a chaise and Carlos leads me over to lounge on it.

"What goes on here?"

Carlos tells me, "This is a space dedicated to your senses. Close your eyes and see if you can identify the sounds."

My hesitancy to close my eyes in a darkened room with a stranger must have shown on my face.

"Nothing will happen without your permission. I promise. You may stop me whenever you like," Carlos tells me.

I close my eyes and soon hear a soft skin on skin sound. The rhythm is unmistakable. The cadence is steady and then increases.

"I'm going to guess it is two people having sex."

"That one is pretty easy," he says. "Let's test your hearing a bit further."

We walk down the hall past other doors until Carlos stops and turns on the intercom. Moaning comes out of the room. A woman is softly saying "More, more, don't stop."

A male voice says, "Put your legs on my shoulders" a rustling sound follows then the steady beat again.

A different woman speaks. "Open your mouth, Claudia. Turn your head this way, Paul." She sounds on the verge.

"I think that must be three people having sex."

"Okay, let's go a little further down the hall to touch."

We go past doors, open and closed into an alcove with a closet and a chaise.

"Clothing is optional. Would you care to undress?" he opens the closet and removes a black silk robe. "You are not forced to do anything and can say stop anytime you wish," he reminds me.

I take the robe and slip off my dress. I stand a minute in my corset and debate with myself if I want to remove it. He is standing, watching and the desire in his eyes makes me slow down. I put the robe across the chaise and have a seat. I watch him remove his white trousers and shirt, along with his sandals. Then I stand to remove my corset and slip into the robe.

"Would you like to guess what you are being touched with," he asks with a sensuous smile

"I don't mind if I do."

"Close your eyes. Remember you can always tell me to stop. Are there any areas off limits?"

"I don't want anything inside of me." I don't want him putting something where it shouldn't go and then having it get stuck.

"Then let's work on the outside." I hear the closet opening and then he opens my robe. I feel a smooth damp sensation on my breasts. It trails from left to right tit and glides smoothly from one to the other and back again.

"Do you know what it is?" he asks as he continues to go back and forth.

"I don't have a clue."

"It's a strip of satin, dipped in oil."

I open my eyes and look at the trail the oil has left on my body. The feeling is luxurious.

"Ready to play again?"

"Yes."

"Close your eyes."

I comply and hear him go to the closet again.

He comes back and whispers in my ear, "What is this?"

Softness circles my breasts then goes down and stops at the bottom of my abdomen. It is getting hot as I answer, "A piece of fur. I take off my robe and so does he.

"You're right. The score is one and one. Open your legs for the tie breaker. What is this?"

I feel his hands opening me before I feel a rough soft sensation on my thighs and then on my pussy. It's large and moves on my nether lips. It could not possibly enter me but it feels unusual. It's not until I feel his breath on my thigh I understand the feeling.

"Damn. Is that your head right there?" I open my eyes to be sure. Sure enough, his head is at my apex like he is being born feet first.

"I guess you win." He kisses me intimately and repeatedly on my intimate place until I am ready to scream. Then he comes up and over me to kiss me long and deeply in my mouth.

He feels right. I like his weight and his size. Should I or shouldn't I? I pull his face down to mine for another kiss then take his very impressive dick in my hand.

"May I?" he politely asks.

"Yes you may" I position him where I want him to be and open wider.

He takes over and gives me a fantastic ride on the D-train I won't soon forget. All thoughts of the frogs I kissed before are swept away, I've found the prince, and he has the equipment and the stamina to take me over the edge three times. When we're finished, I put on the robe and gather my dress and corset.

Carlos gets dressed and asks, "May I come with you to your room?"

If he comes to the room, I'll feel the need to entertain him in addition to not being able to sleep in the middle of the bed. "I prefer to sleep alone." I tell him as I dress.

"Will you be here tomorrow?"

"No, I think I will be leaving tomorrow. Thank you for a wonderful night."

"Thank you as well. Safe journey and if you come back to Monaco, please look me up. He reaches into his trouser pocket and gives me a card.

"May I walk you back to the foyer?" he asks like a true gentleman.

"Please do."

We walk back arm in arm to the main area. Alita is nowhere to be found. I ask Carlos, "Could you take me to the elevator?"

When we get there, he kisses me again. The elevator comes and I get on. "Thank you for a great game Carlos."

"Indeed, it was my pleasure."

I blow him a kiss as the doors close. Back in the room, I get a bath for the second time. Washing off bodily fluids is getting to be a habit. I go to bed and think over my adventure with Carlos. I forgot to use the conversation tips I had got from the friendly exhibitionist. Oh well, maybe next time. I turn out the light and as soon as my head hits the pillow, go to sleep.

In the morning, Alita gets me up early. "Ma petite, we will travel to Liberia soon to meet the Marylanders. We must make it back to France."

"Marylanders?"

"From Maryland County."

"Oh, I was thinking of the state of Maryland. It seems odd there's a Maryland in Liberia."

"Actually Liberia was supported by freed slaves who were sent to Liberia by the American Colonization Society. Unfortunately, they treated the natives as they had been treated by whites in America, changing the names of the people and places to American names. If you were a Liberian privileged enough to stay with them, they did not allow you to speak your dialect because they could not understand it and they felt threatened by conversation. Calling a Liberian a damn native man was the equivalent of calling them a nigger. But we natives are a proud people and we have survived."

"That's good information to have. At least I know what not to say. I'll be ready shortly. What else do I need to know about where we are going?"

"We will then travel to Maryland County. We must ensure that the rituals are performed. Now, come and greet the day."

Recovery from the past two nights is slow. My eyes have seen more live porn in one day than I have seen in fifty years of living. It takes a bit longer than usual to get my things together. Ever efficient, Enufu has us bundled up and heading back to the train station in a very short period of time.

During the train ride to Nice, my thoughts are on the little place we just left. The questions come quickly. "Tell me about the palace. Who runs it, where did you learn about it?"

She gives one of her standard non-answers that says everything and nothing. "Cherie, you meet people, you find places."

"Actually, I'm still a bit shocked by what happened, but I enjoyed the adventure."

Alita smiles and I leave the questioning alone to enjoy the scenery. When we arrive in Nice, Enfu ensures we make it onto the plane for Paris before leaving and going back wherever he stays when Alita is not here.

SWEET LIBERIA

Back in Paris, Etienne meets us at the airport. "I trust your visit went pleasantly."

If I were two shades lighter, my face would have been as red as an apple. I squeeze out, "Yes Etienne, it was a very pleasant trip. I got to see so much of Monaco."

He looks at Alita and they share an open smile. He has us back to the house where Louis comes to get the luggage.

 We spend the day doing last minute shopping. We get small gifts to give, perfume for the women, ink pens and watches for the men. Alita explains the gifts will be given to the village. As they are needed, they will be used.

There is a delicious meal of chicken in white wine sauce with roasted vegetables awaiting us for dinner. The evening runs away and it's soon bedtime.

"Sleep dear one, we have much traveling tomorrow." Alita strokes my cheek and heads off towards her room while I go send an e-mail to my mother.

I go in and throw myself across the bed. The lack of sleep or the energy exerted the past few days soon comes to claim the last vestiges of alertness from my body.

The next morning there is quite a bit of bustling on my part. Etienne is ever present and as calm as Alita. At breakfast I tell Alita, "I'm going to make sure all my packing is complete."

"I shall help Etienne," is her answer.

"It must be great to have someone to smooth the way."

"Yes it makes life much easier. "

"Who will go with us to Liberia?"

"When I am in Africa, I have my family. It would insult them for me to bring along one of my, oh, let's call them assistants. The people there wouldn't understand. They have only now accepted my painting and the fact that it is my chosen profession."

"Oh. I don't mean to be nosey."

"Feel free to ask me anything."

"Thank you, Alita. It helps me to understand."

We separate and I make sure all of my things for Liberia are ready. A few hours later, Louis knocks on the door. My bags are ready and he picks them up.

At the door he turns to say, "I hope you have enjoyed your stay."

"Yes, I most definitely did."

"May you enjoy Liberia also. I am here to assist you upon your return in any way you desire."

"Thank you Louis."

We head out to the airport in the late afternoon for the next part of my adventure, a trip to Liberia. It will take us eight hours with an hour long layover in Casablanca, where we will pick up passengers, but not have to leave the plane. We will arrive in Monrovia at two in the morning.

Once the plane takes off, I ask my mate, "Alita, I would like to know what will happen when we arrive. You've talked quite a bit about ceremony. What do you mean?

Alita laughs. "When we first arrive in Monrovia, there will be a welcoming ceremony. This ritual will occur at a place selected by the Marylanders in Monrovia."

"What will happen there?"

"Everyone will be outside. The men will be sitting in a circle and the women and children will be outside of the circle. Some of the older women may come into the circle if they are considered strong in the community. As we sit and wait for everyone to be seated, people will come and shake our hand. They will ask you your name and it is important that you answer. Do you remember the question as it will sound in dialect?"

"I think so."

"Very good. Then they will tell you their name. After a period of time, someone will rise and call everyone's attention. After the call to attention, the chief will stand and order the serving of the cola and pepper. The purpose of the cola and pepper is to welcome strangers. The cola is hard and bitter. The pepper is ground hot pepper pods.

If you would prefer not to eat, dip your finger in the water that covers the cola and lick the water from your finger. If you choose to eat the cola, you will pick up a small piece, dip it into the ground pepper and eat it."

"Will they be offended if I choose not to eat the pepper?"

 "No, they will not be offended, but if you choose to eat the cola and pepper, you will gain their respect. After they serve the cola and pepper, there will be another person who will have a pitcher of water and a glass, yet another will have bottle and a glass.

First you will be offered water. That is a show of purity and good intent. Then you will be offered cane juice, which is what your people call moonshine, to quench the thirst. The pourers will go around the entire circle with the glass and offer some to each person. All will share from the same glass. You may drink the amount poured for you, decline, or accept your portion and pour it onto the ground."

"Why would I pour it onto the ground? What a waste, even though I don't drink moonshine, I don't want to waste any."

"For the ancestors, for those who have gone before. They cannot drink so the ground drinks for them. After the drinking is complete, the servers will place the cola, pepper, water and cane juice on a table in front of the leader. The leader will then ask me why we are here. I will answer by explaining we have come to bury their brother and tell them you are my mate and also come to say goodbye. After the leader hears this, he will say words of blessing and there will be food. Then everyone will come together to eat."

"The eating shouldn't be a problem."

Alita smiles. "We shall see. When we travel to Cape Palmas or Maryland, we will spend one night in Harper and then go to Middletown. In Harper there will be a similar ceremony, and yet another in Middletown."

"That's quite a bit of ceremony for one man," I comment.

"But what a man, no?"

"What a man, yes," I tell her as my lips turn into a smile at the memory of him.

"The actual false burial ceremony will be in Middletown."

"I'm glad it's not like a funeral pyre where the wife has to throw herself on top. I like you and would hate to see you burn. And I definitely do not want me to burn."

"No Lynn, we won't be burning,"

"Will I have to do anything?"

"I will explain more when we arrive there. Once you have seen some of our ceremony, it will make more sense. You may participate as you wish. Do not feel you must do anything."

We both fall silent and I must have fallen asleep because I wake up when the cabin crew starts moving through the airplane waking people up with their noise. A look to my right shows Alita is staring straight ahead; as she was when I last looked at her. As if sensing my return to consciousness, she turns to look at me and smiles.

"Na wie oh." Hello.

I bet she thinks I don't remember the response. "Ma ye ah." I meet you.

"Na fe dey." How is your body?

The words seem awkward and I'm sure the pronunciation is off, but this is not my primary language.

"Na fe nu tay." "I am doing fine," she tells me.

"The people of Middletown will appreciate your taking the time to learn something. Do you remember what you are to say when someone says Ah bi si Nie Swa?"

"I tell God thank you."

"Lynn, you will do well in our home."

"I hope I don't disappoint."

"Be yourself and allow yourself to shine." Alita reaches over and strokes my face.

The plane is touching down and we are given last minute instructions. We eventually get to take off our seat bells and retrieve our luggage from the overhead compartments.

As the doors open, the African heat rushes in to smack me in the face. The humidity takes my breath away and starts me sweating. Alita has nothing but her purse. She bends slightly and retrieves it from under the seat in front of her. She moves out into the aisle and heads toward the front of the plane.

I get my overnight bag and purse then follow as best as I can. We are soon separated from each other by the crush of people coming out of the seats into the aisle. I am waiting in the line to disembark and the excitement to get off the plane and see the motherland increases. Little old me, in Africa. Some ancestor of mine may have been in this same location only a couple of hundred years in the past. And now I am here sweating like I'm about to be sold. Damn this heat is killing me and I haven't spent the first hour here.

At the door, there is no huge tube to take us into the terminal. We must go down a set of roll away stairs that go in a steep straight line to the ground. I get a death grip on the rail with one hand and try to descend with my overnight bag and purse in the other hand. The gentleman in front of me is alerted to possible disaster when I scream. I almost missed a step and the possibility of falling causes me to warn all of the people in front of me.

I see Alita look at me. Her smile pisses me off.

"HELP! I'm going to die." My feet are wobbling and Alita is moving down the stairs as if she is walking on air.

"No you're not." She tosses over her shoulder.

The kind gentleman who would take the first hit from my fall turns. He sees my knuckles and the abject terror that must show on my face and offers to take my bag down. Once free of my overnight bag, and with a hand on each side of the stair rails, I feel definitely safer. Inch by inch the descent to the bottom is eventually complete. It matters little if there is an almost full plane full of people waiting to get past me, self preservation is important. I hear Alita's laughter from in front of me.

At the bottom, my steps are slightly faster, but not by much. I do have my eyes more open now and look around to get a glimpse of a stray elephant, tiger, or zebra on the runway. But scans of the area reveal nothing more exciting than a nondescript building swallowing up the other passengers from my flight. Except for a few floodlights, it is pitch black out here. So much for knowing you were having company and leaving a light on for them. The crowd has excellent night vision and gathers me to surge toward the building. Mr. Nice Guy returns my overnight bag and I kindly thank him for his assistance.

"No mind," he tells me. "Will you be in Liberia for long?" His accent makes his speech smooth and lilting.

"Uhh." He could be trying to steal my identity.

"We stay for a week," Alita answers as she appears at my elbow.

"I am here for two weeks. Perhaps dinner one night?"

"Uhh." He must be talking to Alita even though his eyes are directed towards me.

"Lynn has a busy schedule, but here is our direction. She would be happy to go to dinner one night I am sure. I am Alita." Alita gives him the card that appears in her hand.

"And here is mine," he responds and takes my hand to put a card there. He folds my fingers around it, smiles, and turns to enter the building.

"Why did you give him a card, Alita? We don't know him."

She gives her trademark shrug and replies, "You meet people, you meet people. And it's past time for you to meet people."

We continue forward and enter Roberts International Airport, the largest airport in Liberia. It is probably the only airport in Liberia, and this is definitely not the JFK airport. It isn't as big as the airport in Wichita. I pass through the double doors and see two signs. One says Liberian and ECOWAS members with an arrow pointing to the left side and another sign reads "Other Nationalities" pointing to the right side of the large room.

"What is an ECOWAS Alita? "

"It is the union of West African States. People from those countries can travel freely between the countries without a visa."

"I guess that makes me an 'Other Nationalities'."

"Right. I will see you in the baggage claim area in a few minutes.

"If I don't get lost."

"You can't get lost in this little place. Just show them your visa and you'll be done soon."

"See you in a few minutes, Alita."

The room for Other Nationalities has a row of five teller windows. It is quickly filling up and I jump in what seems to be the smallest line.

My turn at the window finally comes.

"Where do you come from?" the immigration officer asks me.

"I'm from Kansas."

"What brings you to Liberia?" she wants to know.

"I'm here with a friend for a false burial."

"It sure is hot," she shares as if she is imparting a well kept secret.

"Yes, it is. I'm sweating," I tell her in case she thinks the water on my face is rain.

"Some cold water would be nice."

"It sure would," I say in agreement.

"Or a Coke."

"I prefer Pepsi myself, but Coke would be fine too," I say in an effort to be agreeable.

"A nice cold Coke" she continues with a slight scowl.

"I guess." Maybe each country has its own soft drink loyalty. Liberia must be on the side of Coke in the cola wars.

She is still holding my passport and people on all sides of me are passing on through the door while the talking machine is giving me the weather report and her idea of the best refreshment.

I decide to stop talking and give her the opportunity to do her job. I stare at her. Instead of putting the stamp in my passport like the other tellers at the windows, she is looking back at me.

Finally, she stands and says, "Ma'am, come through the door and follow me."

What the heck? Did I fail some type of unwritten test?

"Why, what did I do?" I ask as nice as possible for me to ask after traveling way too long.

"Please do not make a scene. Come through the door." She motions to a narrow door on the opposite wall from the door everyone else is going through.

I shouldn't have mentioned Pepsi at all. They take this cola war too seriously. I turn around and look for Alita, but she is nowhere to be found. Robert may be right. It would have been better not to have come here.

Maybe the nice man who helped me get down the steps put something in my overnight bag. But I still have my bag, so they didn't check it and find anything. Maybe it is something in my passport. The only countries in my passport are Mexico, Canada, France and Monaco. Liberia isn't at war with any of them. Even if they are, I didn't take sides.

I walk towards the door she holds open for me to enter the bowels of the Liberian immigration department. We enter a smaller room with three doors. The immigration officer is preparing to speak to me when one of the doors opens. A short round man comes out and stops when he sees the immigration officer and me.

"What is the problem here?" he says in a short man's booming voice

"Chief, I was not aware you were here."

"But what is the problem?" he asks again.

"This American woman," she says with a jut of her chin in my direction.

"Hey, wait a minute, I'm not a problem." They both ignore me.

"Where are her papers?"

"Here they are, Chief."

They speak quickly in a dialect with much gesturing and many looks in my direction.

He takes my passport and starts back towards the door he came out of.

"Excuse me. You have my passport."

"Come with me," barks the short little bastard.

When I enter, he shuts the door behind me, closing me in an office the size of a small bedroom. Shorty takes his seat, his napoleon complex evident in the size of his desk. He could lie on top of it and stretch his arms over his head and not touch either end.

There is a chair in front of his desk. He doesn't bother to offer it to me. I stand while he makes a production of looking at my passport. I stand in silence for three minutes by my watch. The thought of the trees in Sedona cross my mind and get my feet moving to cross the room and sit in the seat opposite him. He looks up but refuses to say a word.

I'm grouchy and not sure why he brought me here. As I sit, the mountains in Sedona, Arizona remain in my mind. They were majestic. What would the mountains think of my present situation?

"What seems to be the problem and why did you bring me here?" I ask him politely.

"It seems you do not have the appropriate visa."

"How can that be when I obtained the visa in the United States before leaving? Your embassy in Washington issued the visa and I even paid extra to have my visa expedited." I am a mountain and this little person is not going to intimidate me.

"I do not see it here."

"Then you must be mistaken. I saw the visa several times. Hand me my passport and I'll show it to you."

There is a commotion in the outer room seconds before the door flies open and hits the wall with a resounding bang. Alita enters. Shorty stands and looks at her. The blood drains from his face leaving him gray.

"What is the meaning of this? Why do you have my mate in your office," she demands.

"Na kne?" he croaks. Are you living?

"Na kne na edy ye," Alita speaks firmly. I'm living, yes.

"So sorry madam. We have delayed you from your mission here. The stupid girl that brought you here, I will fire her," he turns to tell me.

"Do not act the innocent. The corruption of the immigration office here is known even in France." Alita stridently states as she walks towards his desk.

"Too bad I didn't know about it in Kansas."

"Sorry sorry, madam. This is a mistake. It will be corrected immediately," he tells me.

He is holding the passport out to me and Alita snatches it from his shaking hand.

"I shall not quickly forget this insult," Alita tells him.

Sweat is on his face as he attempts to explain. "But it was an accident."

"There was no accident. The president will be informed," Alita tells him as she gently pushes me in front of her to exit the office. She snaps the door shut on his protestations of innocence and pleas for mercy.

"Alita what was that all about?"

"He wanted a bribe to do his job. Unfortunately, bribery happens far too often and is not in the best interest of the country and that hurts the economy. I forgot to warn you about the corruption. I wasn't thinking."

"Will you tell the president? Do you know the president?"

"Are you hurt?"

"No, not hurt, just confused."

"Then no. I will not tell the president, he would lose his job. I want him to do better and not harass the visitors. How are you doing?"

"It was scary. I didn't know what was happening. Then I thought about strength and channeled that strength. I was kind of proud of myself."

"No mind Lynn, it was my fault for not warning you of the corruption." Alita leads the way to a waiting jeep. There is a young man standing beside the open door tipping his hat.

"Welcome, welcome auntie. Thank you," he tells me.

"Thank you for what?" I don't think I did anything.

"For coming to Liberia. I am Joseph."

"Oh. You're welcome. It's very nice to meet you Joseph." I climb into the back of the car and Alita comes in after me.

It isn't until after we get into the waiting car, which already holds our luggage. I remember she didn't tell me if she knows the president.

"We will go to Maude Barclay Estates, Joseph," she tells the driver.

"So do you know the president?" I ask her.

"You know people, you know people," is her answer to me.

We drive through streets needing the attention of someone to fill the potholes big enough to swallow large dogs. There is very little traffic until we arrive at a busy intersection. Then there are people and cars congesting the traffic in a way that would make New York City seem empty. This is definitely a twenty-four hour town.

"What is this place, Alita?"

"It is the new campus for the university. The main campus is still located across from the Capital building, but this campus was needed so educational activities can continue to flourish in our little country." Her pride is evident in every word.

Joseph turns onto a small road and drives until we reach a brick wall where he honks and a teen youth comes to open a wrought iron gate. We pull into the wide yard with a circular driveway. It reminds me of Alita's driveway in France. The façade of the home is also similar and the stairway has the same markings and decorations. Joseph jumps out and opens the door for us to exit. The front door is opened by a short caramel colored girl with a striped shirt and a multi printed wrap around skirt.

She runs into Alita's arms as she speaks in rapid dialect and English ending with "Mommy Alita, you are here."

"Yes Woapla, I am here," Alita answers as she returns the hug.

Another young girl in a tie dyed dress exits. She is much shorter and darker than Woapla and she also runs to Alita speaking only in dialect.

Alita admonishes her while giving her a hug. "English, Wilhelmina, English,"

"I am happy to see you Mommy Alita."

"Come Lynn, meet the young ladies. Woapla, Willie, make yourselves known to Auntie Lynn."

The two of them look at me before coming forward to take my hand and say their name. They clearly want to be with Alita and I don't blame them. She has the magnetic personality that causes people to gravitate towards her. No wonder her children feel it also.

"Alita, I thought you didn't have children?"

"My children? Oh Willie and Woapla. They are mine inasmuch as they live here and I provide for them. But they are our children. You are a part of the family it will take to raise them." She turns to Woapla to say, "You are responsible for Auntie Lynn. You must give her every assistance while she is here. She is family."

Woapla nods and comes to stand at my side. "I shall help in any way I can."

I smile and take her hand, ready to give them the catching up time they want with Alita. "I would really like to see my room and start unpacking. I can stretch the kinks out from the flight and get some sleep. Can Woapla show me to my room?" The sweat is intolerable, and the heat is something like the inside of a hothouse.

"Of course you must refresh yourself. Are you hungry?" she asks with a young lady in each arm.

"No, just tired."

"In the morning we will go to waterside and purchase material for you to have some things made," Alita informs me.

"Some dresses," I ask remembering my meager packing.

"Lappa suits. You would call them wrap around skirts, but here the lappa is the native skirt. The tops are made of the same material and there is often material for the head wrap to complete your ensemble."

"Okay. Shopping in the morning," I agree.

Woapla leads me to the door of the house before asking Alita, "Where will she sleep?"

"Put her in the suite. This is her home too and she must be comfortable."

I go into a door to the left of the front room we entered to find myself in a sitting room with a couch, two easy chairs, and artwork on every wall. Pictures of Mr. M.O.P. in different poses, some with Alita at his side and some with band members playing in various venues.

I recognize Alita's work and appreciate the detail she put into every brush stroke. There is an intense rendering of the two of them, obviously quite young and dressed in matching fabric.

Woapla notices my perusal and asks "The old ma is very talented, no?"

"The old ma is very talented yes." Her work is arresting. The attention to detail gives the expectation he will speak to me at any moment.

Woapla leads me into another room with bookcases, a desk and chair, and a small refrigerator. The bed is huge enough for me to sleep in the middle sideways without falling out.

Woapla is struggling to get the clothing unpacked and I stop her.

"Dear, I can do the unpacking. I am sure you want to go and talk with Alita. I'll take care of this."

"But my job is to care for you."

"And you've done a wonderful job. If I need anything at all, I'll come and get you, okay? Why don't you go out and talk to Alita?"

Her face lights up and she runs to turn down the bed and fluff the pillows before saying, "Rest well Auntie Lynn."

I walk around the suite, getting familiar with everything. I decide to test the bed and go over to fall face first into heaven. I close my eyes and block out everything in hopes I will feel cooler. It helps and soon I am asleep.

The next morning the growl of my stomach wakes me up. The need to dress is secondary to the need to appease my appetite so I throw on a wrap and go straight to the breakfast table. It is set for three and I wonder who the third attendee will be. There are six covered bowls on the table.

Woapla appears at the door to the dining room and stands silently. We look at each other. She is a very short girl about four feet six inches with a round face and a beautiful smile. She stands quietly while I wonder if I am supposed to say something. She speaks first

"May I get something for you to drink, hot water for coffee?

As hot as it is, why does she think I would want to drink coffee? "Thank you so much, but do you have anything else?"

"I can get you some hot chocolate or some beer," she offers.

Hot chocolate when it's hot enough to cause sand to sweat or beer after last night and before eight in the morning doesn't sound appealing. "How about something cold without alcohol," I ask her.

"I can make some butter plum juice."

"Sounds tasty."

While she's getting the liquid, it's time to investigate the food by looking under the dish covers. The first contains boiled eggs. The second has oatmeal pale enough to benefit from some butter and brown sugar. The third has sausages and the fourth has pineapple. The fifth bowl has grits and the last one has bread.

I consider waiting on Alita to come eat for about three seconds before the pineapple begs me to take a sample. My fork poised to spear a chunk when the door opens and the bearer of fluid enters.

"May I fix your plate?"

"No thank you, Woapla, I'll get it." My fork sinks into a pineapple piece juicy enough to send juices squirting across the table.

Alita enters looking like she had slept in air conditioning.

"Good morning. Did you sleep peacefully?" She asks.

"It was rather warm, but I tried."

"Ah yes the heat. You will adjust. Woapla, may I have coffee please?"

She slides into the chair and Woapla, our drink person, slips out.

Alita fills her plate and when she lifts her fork to her mouth, Woapla slips back in with a steaming cup of coffee. She pours milk from the can sitting on the table and puts in two cubes of sugar. After stirring, Woapla sits the saucer and cup at Alita's left. Alita picks up the cup and sips. With a smile on her face she looks at Woapla.

"Very well done. Is it not time for you to prepare for school?"

"Boku Weah says I must stay from school and help with the quee woman."

I look around, unaware there were other guests staying here.

"No ma petite, it is a must you tend to your education. Ensure breakfast is ready early every day and then you go to school. Your education is critical."

Woapla dips a curtsey and heads out of the room.

"Alita, how many relatives are living here?"

"Everyone is related dear one. Woapla is the relative of our husband. She is here so she can go to school. She will take care of the cooking in the morning and will fix dinner for us while we are here."

"So you support her?"

"This is a family home. Anyone needing shelter is welcome. When anyone, friends or family, comes, they can stay here while they determine what path they choose, work or school. Weah, my cousin, takes care of other things. He comes once a week if no one is here and more often if there is someone in residence."

"How would he know someone was here?"

"Woapla will send word to him if someone arrives. If Woapla is at school, there is a spare key under the foot pad on the porch. You are welcome here since the house was built by our husband."

I think about how dangerous it is to have a key under the mat on the porch in the United States. It would probably be safe in Wichita and the idea makes me laugh.

"So what will we do today, Alita?"

"We will go to the county association here in Monrovia. It is customary to show ourselves so we will be welcomed and not slight the people of my county. We like pomp and circumstance you see, so we will start our visit here."

"What time does it start?"

"There is a meeting at five o'clock this evening. Before then we will go to waterside and shop."

"What should I wear?"

"Be comfortable. We will be there for quite a time."

"Okay."

I go back to my room and look for something comfortable. It would probably be easier if the sweat from my head wasn't dripping into my eyes. There is a valley between my breasts where a creek is running into the beginning of a creek at the top of my thighs. Hot doesn't begin to describe the weather.

My hand goes to the baby wipes with aloe vera. As the cool moisture is applied, a soothing feeling envelopes the skin touched with aloe. Unfortunately, there isn't enough to bathe in, so my body has to settle for a wipe down which feels calming and encourages me to dress in loose clothing.

Wilhelmina comes to the door to tell me, "It is time to go to waterside and shop."

Alita is on the porch and the car is in front. While we ride Alita tells me our shopping plan of attack.

"You will choose some fabric for three or four outfits. We will first go to my designer. One outfit should be black, the others should be colorful."

"Why black?"

"Remember when we first arrive for the false burial, we will don the black outfit to pay homage to our departed husband and symbolize our loss. The next day will be the day for colors and the day we have the cutting of the hair and selection of a new husband. Everyone will dress wearing their best clothes. The widows of the man are expected to cut their hair to show their love for the husband or select a new husband."

Looking at Alita's dreads, hanging down her back and touching her ass, it occurs to me maybe I didn't love him as much as she does. I don't want to give up my shoulder length twists to prove to a bunch of strangers I cared for him. "Alita, about this hair cutting thing... I don't want to get married, or to have my hair cut."

"It's symbolism. The cutting of the hair is to show your grief at your loss. But don't worry Lynn, don't worry. We will not have our hair cut. The hair will be paid for. We can buy it ourselves or a suitor from the family can purchase it for us. I have no desire to have my head shaved either" she tells me as she takes a long rope of hair in her hand. "The money will go to the village coffers and his honor will be maintained."

"How much hair will be cut?" My hand goes to twist my twists and my eyes travel to Alita's dreadlocks.

"The woman's head is completely shaved."

"Damn. That's rather drastic. I definitely don't want my head shaved." I can just imagine me going home bald as a biscuit. What a load off my mind. Now as to getting married again, that's not really what I had in mind when I came. Marriage didn't work out so well for me the first time."

"Do not concern yourself with choosing a husband. You may look at the members of his family and decide if any will suit you. If so, you will select him. If not, you may leave the family. Who knows, maybe one of the males will consider you worthy"

"Then what would happen."

"If the women are considered worthy, the males in the family will declare their interest by putting bamboo sticks in the hair of the widows. If she keeps the stick in her hair, she accepts the suitor. He pays for her hair and it is not cut. After a period of time, they will marry."

"But Alita what if she doesn't want anyone in the family? I certainly am not looking for a husband."

"If she doesn't want anyone in the family, she leaves her children and goes back to her family."

"She has to leave her children?"

"Yes. She came into the marriage without children. In our custom, the children belong to the man and they are for his family if the wife leaves."

"What if she doesn't want to remarry or leave her children?"

"She can decide to stay with the family of her husband, but she is not allowed to have another man. At a certain age, the woman may also decide to select her husband. We will talk more about that later. The next day is the division of the assets of the departed. "

"Will you select a new husband from among his family members?"

"Most assuredly," Alita laughs then explains. "I have no desire to have another husband to attempt to control me. I shall select one of the younger boys as my husband. This will keep the family intact and allow me my freedom."

"One of the younger boys. How young?" There must be laws against what she is proposing to do to some poor innocent child.

"Someone under ten. Then my responsibility will be to educate him and raise him more as a son. The need for symbolism is met and our husband is honored by my desire to remain a part of his family. Our husband was extremely proud of his native roots, in this way I continue his legacy while ensuring the education of the next generation."

"Can I do the same thing? I didn't want to cut my hair, but I want to honor the impact he had on my life by making a difference in the life of his descendants."

"I would be honored, as would he, if you chose to do so."

WHAT'S ON WATERSIDE

Joseph arrives at the shopping location. He pulls over on the side of a street at the top of a hill with a sloping sidewalk leading down to the water. On both sides of the crowded street are shops and goods to be purchased. Outside on the sidewalk are children and adults standing holding goods fabric, toothbrushes, watches and everything else imaginable for sell. Inside the doors there are tempting displays hanging on the walls. It is quite a bit to process.

"Hold tightly to your purse," Alita tells me as we exit and start down the sidewalk. The people are haggling and conversations abound. I look in storefronts with jewelry, ivory carvings, leather briefcases, and rubber shoes. It seems anything is available at waterside. Fabric stores are plentiful and Alita laughs at my enjoyment. We finally enter a fabric store where the owner immediately rushes over to us.

"My dear Alita, so wonderful to see you," he gives her a hug and turns to me with a questioning look.

"Hello Twan. This is my mate, Lynn. We need to select some fabric for her false burial clothing."

"I have the perfect fabric, it is very fine."

He rushes towards the back and returns with yards of lacy black print with sequins sewn in a bird pattern repeated down the middle.

My hand goes to touch it and it's easy to say, "This is beautiful."

"I guess we have the material for the false burial then. Now we must get some fabric for a few other outfits," Alita says.

We wander around the shop to find the right fabric. Alita helps me to judge if the fabric works with my skin tones, something new and exciting for me. She drapes the fabric under my chin and we look in the mirror. The colors she helps me select make me look alive. I choose peacock blue, salmon, and pink with white netting using the same method. To dress in vibrant colors instead of the usual shades of brown and earth tones Robert approved for me is energizing.

Alita gets a bright yellow fabric with black design, a purple with pink dots and a black with cream shot through. Alita declares, "Now we must go to my designer and select some styles."

"The cost is so reasonable it seems wasteful not to get more." My hand goes forward to stroke a vibrant red lacy piece of fabric. We hold it up to my face.

Alita asks me, "What do you think?"

"It looks awful," I laughingly tell her. I look around for another possibility.

She stops me by saying, "Remember all of the stores we passed? You will want to shop there also. This store will be here if you want to come back later."

We pay Twan and he calls a young man to carry our fabric. Alita and I head back up the hill past small shops with rows of sewing machines. There is clothing hanging in every available space on the walls. At the top of the hill we enter a store where a tall distinguished looking man comes forward.

"Alita, I am honored" he kisses her on both cheeks.

"Well met, Francis. I have brought my mate and we need clothing, two outfits each for tomorrow."

Francis is a slight man, black as the inside of a tire. His pearly white teeth and twinkling eyes make me smile in return.

"Come sit, come sit. And you expect me to have them ready overnight, right Mrs. Alita?"

"I would not be here otherwise. Is it possible?"

"You are correct, it will be as you desire." Francis pulls a tape measure and paper from a drawer in his sewing machine stand. "Let me get some measurements. There are style books for you to select how you want the fabric made. Lappa suits for you both?"

"Oui, lappa suits. Measure Lynn first, I have not changed."

He has numbers for my arms, skirt length, bust, and waist. Then he allows me to look at pictures to select something perfect. Alita has already selected something and she talks to Francis while I peruse the pictures. Finally, a design with lovely sleeves and a plunging neckline screams for me to choose it for the black, another with a more demure neckline and long billowy sleeves is perfect for the pink with white netting. The blue will have short puffed sleeves and buttons down the front. All will have the long lappa skirt and a head wrap.

We also purchase some tie-dye dresses with embroidered fronts. They look comfortable enough for travel. Afterwards, we head to other stores on waterside. The crowd presses in from most sides and to escape, I wander around inside a store.

There are rows and rows of necklaces with graduated beads made of ivory and with carvings of people, dice, and animals. Some of the larger pieces have scenes of village life carved into the bead.

I take a colorful strand of beads. Like the others, it looks slightly unfinished because of the long string hanging on either end. I turn to ask Alita her opinion.

"Do you like this necklace? I know it ties at the end and all of the string is distracting, but overall, I like the little beads."

"Lynn, that is not a necklace."

"What is it then?"

"It is used by women to hold their under cloth in place. The idea of lingerie, as you know it, is not what is worn in the interior. The women take cloth and hold it up with these beads. Young girls have small beads. As the female gets older, the size of the beads increases. To wear this as a necklace would be the same as putting your panties around your neck."

"Oh."

I look at some of the larger styles. They are equally colorful. I am reminded of the gold chains Alita had used and how sensuous it was to wear them. I kept the one around my waist after I had returned home. It was the last vestiges of my time with our husband I removed. Even now I have it on. But it's time to put an end to his time in my life.

"Alita, I'm going to get some. I like the idea."

She smiles and joins me in selecting an emerald green set with cream stripes. "We will put it on you when we return home. For a man to feel these beads is an honor."

"Well I doubt I'll find anyone to feel them, but I'll know they're there."

Other stores have shoes, others handbags made of lizard. It is a kaleidoscope of color and people milling around being a part of the scene. Soon, we have purchased everything we need and quite a few things we don't need.

We get our purchases home and Alita, true to her word comes to help me put on my beads. They hang low on my hips and I like the feel of them. The heat is draining so it makes sense to take a nap. Alita tells me she is also going to take a nap after she has the opportunity to talk more with Woapla and Wilhelmina

"Do you want me to call the gentleman you met at the airport?"

"No Alita, I don't think I'm ready to meet anyone now."

"Well, here is his card. You may call before you leave and at least say hello."

"I'll think about it."

When she is gone, I put my feet up on the bed, glad to give them a reprieve from all of the walking we had done. The door opening brings me back to consciousness.

"It is almost time to go to the county meeting. Woapla informs me.

A glance at the clock shows the time is ten minutes until five. It only takes me a few minutes to dress then head to the living room. Alita is sitting without a drop of sweat, dressed in a flowing blue lace caftan. The kitten heel sandals on her feet look as comfortable as she does.

"Cherie, are you ready?"

"Have you been waiting long? So sorry to be late."

"There is no problem; we will arrive when it is time."

"But I thought it starts at five?"

"The concept of time is a bit different here. It actually started at four. We must not arrive exactly on time, they should be assembled and we will enter for them to see us."

"Why are we going again?"

"So the people here can express their condolences. Our husband was well known so many will pay homage."

"Oh."

"Come we will leave now."

The drive to the meeting takes us thirty minutes through streets dappled with potholes large enough to swallow motorcycles. In some places the streets are sparsely populated. In others, people are shoulder to shoulder.

"It is very crowded in some places and empty in others, Alita."

"There is a shortage of vehicles in the city. Everyone is trying to get a taxi or hoping they see someone they know to get a lift."

I people watch a while longer and then ask Alita, "Tell me something about him."

"I wondered how long before your curiosity would overwhelm you. We have spoken of many things, but never of him. Why do you ask now?"

"I feel closest to him now, here where he lived. How long did you know him?"

"We grew together from childhood. He was the third son of the chief of the village. As such, he was expected to marry into a certain strata within our small community. My family had such a status. He was older than I, but from an early age we loved. You will see our village when we go to the Cape Palmas. Our parents did not think we would suit each other after we let them know we intended to be together. They found it easier to give in than to attempt to keep us apart."

"Tell me about his early years."

"He was precocious, inquisitive, mischievous and totally committed to the music. He played the drums for events within the village as soon as he was old enough. Before then he would hang around the drummers watching them. Since he was not the eldest, he was not groomed to takeover and be the town chief."

"Are his brothers still living?"

"No they are gone."

"Did the two of you live in Monrovia for very long?"

"Yes in the same family home we are in now. Indeed, you are sleeping in his room."

"Are there more wives besides you and the one in Maryland?"

"No there are no more. She is a lovely lady, we worked well together to keep peace and to keep him happy. However, she has no desire to leave the village. Her world consisted of raising her children, but not leaving even to come to Monrovia, much less outside of Liberia. He and I needed more than the village had to offer."

"Will we meet her?"

"She remains in the village. Most assuredly, she will meet us there to celebrate the life of our husband."

"What has she been doing?"

"Raising her children and grandchildren. We speak on a regular basis."

"So you were the first wife and you chose her to be the second wife? Why?"

"I chose her to be my mate because of her tremendous commitment to family. I knew early that motherhood was not my forte."

"How many children did he have?"

"We have three children. They are all adults. Woapla is one of our granddaughters."

"What did his family think about him leaving?"

"It's funny you should ask. His grandmother used to come to the door of our home and cry. She said people who know too much leave and do not come back. Therefore they do not know where their family is buried. But we left the village and Liberia."

"Do you still have relatives here?"

"You will meet my cousin today. Weah is a rather interesting character. He will be at the meeting. Now, more questions and answers later. We are here."

Out of the car window, there is a large one story home with cars parked haphazardly and children gathered on the porch. A teenage male with beautiful eyes comes running to open the door for me while the driver opens the door for Alita. He speaks to me in rapid English.

"Hello old mom." He then turns to Alita and with adoration shining in his eyes says, "Thank you for coming. Mother Alita. Thank you."

Alita allows him to reach her side and pay homage with a kiss on the cheek. "You are doing well now Samuel?"

"Yes ma'am. I am attending the university. My grades are the deuce in the class."

His excitement at attending the University of Liberia continues as he talks exclusively to Alita for ten more minutes. He remembers my and existence turns to me.

"I am Samuel," he says and extends his hand.

"Very nice to meet you," I tell him as I extend a hand to shake.

"Samuel is more of the family I told you about. He will make our people proud."

The young man beams as though she just crowned him king.

She encourages him, "You must continue to do well. Our people depend on you."

"I will I promise." He shakes our hand again and moves away.

"Come Lynn we will go to the rear and take part n the meeting."

We walk around to the back of the house and enter an area third the size of a football field surrounded by trees. The aromas of the fruit hanging within hand's reach blending with the scent of the food are enough to make me hungry. The space is populated by a large crowd of people, mostly male sitting in a circle on various chairs and benches. The circle of people part and allow us to enter and to stand next to a short man with ebony black skin and hazel brown eyes. He is wearing a suit coat in spite of the heat with dress pants and slippers on his feet.

Once we are seated, the procession begins. There is a long line that starts at the seat of the chief. After the greeting to the chief each person makes their way towards us. One by one, people leave their seat and come to speak with Alita and then to me. Each one shakes Alita's hand and asks her how she is feeling.

Alita, obviously familiar with the system, shakes the hand and asks after a family member, friend or mutual acquaintance. After speaking with her, they come to me and hold out their hand for a shake. The routine remains the same and my confidence is growing by leaps and bounds. I am actually enjoying myself. Then the mosquitoes start biting. After every handshake I have to slap my arm or my leg to kill a bloodthirsty insect.

The hair on the back of my neck lifts and despite the heat, goose bumps appear on my arms. I have the feeling someone is watching me which doesn't make sense because everyone is watching me.

But this is a different kind of energy. The smile is fixed on my lips as my eyes scan those mulling around the circle. There is one man standing a head above the others.

He has piercing eyes above a wide flat nose that flares as he breathes. His full beard and mustache are black except for the gray that cuts a two inch swath down the middle of his chin. Traveling up his face I watch his nose as it flares when he exhales and inhales. His chest expands and makes me wonder what it would feel like. His eyes are burning a hole in me with their intensity. He doesn't blink and his brown orbs hold no warmth. His mouth is a straight line and his rigid posture has me searching my memory. A deep search doesn't turn up a past meeting with him. I would never have forgotten him.

Finally he blinks and the spell breaks. He starts over to the circle in a straight line for Alita although he never takes his eyes off of me. People move aside and allow him to pass even though he doesn't acknowledge anyone.

He stops in front of my mate and she gives a little squeak before jumping up and throwing her arms around his neck. His eyes warm and his lips bend as he accepts and returns her embrace. He bends to her ear and speaks low and quickly but never moves his eyes from me. Alita looks over at me and answers him with more words than my limited "how's the body" "we thank God" "my name is Lynn" grasp of the language can follow.

Their spirited back and forth stops when she takes his hand and turns him my way. With each step closer I start to feel anxious and my extra perkies point towards him like dart tips to a bulls-eye. All of the other people came on their own to test my knowledge of their dialect so I figure he must be special for Alita to hold his to speed him my way. The mosquitoes take a sabbatical.

"Lynn, this is Weah." Someone else comes to Alita and she continues the handshaking.

Weah doesn't say a word so I tell him, "Hello" and hold out my hand for a shake. I get a blank stare for my troubles. "How are you?" Still nothing except a hostile stare. I switch to dialect. "Na we oh."

He speaks rapidly in his dialect as he takes my hand and holds it limply in his much larger hand. His harsh tone seems angry but I don't understand a damn thing he said. Then he squeezes my hand too hard for comfort before dropping it as if it was covered in chicken shit and closing his mouth. The only thing to be happy about is for a short period of time, the mosquitoes have forgotten my existence

"I'm sorry, my dialect is rather limited." I'd have to be native born to understand all the sounds that had come from his mouth.

He grunts at me before he speaks again, adding gestures in Alita's direction, then starts to walk away. Alita is busy with a long talker and looks quizzically at him for a brief moment. She opens her mouth to speak before he cuts her off with more foreign words. He casts another "kiss my ass" look at me before he turns and goes back the way he had come, with the crowd parting before him.

"Alita, Weah sure is a grumpy person," I tell her when her she is finished talking.

"He has much responsibility and he takes his position seriously. He is usually much friendlier."

"Oh is he the one that watches the home, the one who said Woapla should watch me?"

Alita smiles. "Yes."

"Well he certainly seems bossy." He is standing over at the edge of the crowd watching me. I'm glad he can't hear me, not that it would make a difference since he doesn't speak English. The light painful feel of blood being drawn out of my arm let me know the mosquitoes are at me again.

Another wave of people come and shake my hand and ask my name. I remember to uphold my end of the conversation by asking their name and how they are doing. For some unknown reason my eyes repeatedly find Weah's as they bore a hole in me. His bare arms cross and his face remains unsmiling. I resist the urges to check my teeth for stray food or stick my tongue out at his disapproving glare.

"Bey, Bey, Bey." The loud piercing call comes from an old man stooped and leaning heavily on a cane. It signals the group and people start heading to their seat when he makes the call again. Once everyone is seated, the old man calling everyone to attention is the only one still standing. He takes a horse tail and points around the circle. "Bey, bey, bey" he points the horsetail at the members of the circle as he speaks before shouting, "Dacon a batio"

The crowd responds "Bati."

The man repeats the gesture and call three times. The crowd responds three times then everyone is quiet. The man with the horse tail announces, "It is time to share the cola."

A man comes around with chunks of what looks like white cheese on a white plate with water covering the bottom. Beside the chunks is smeared pepper paste. I copy the movements of others and take a small piece of cola and dip it into the pepper. The cola is hard and bitter. The taste is not helped by adding pepper. When the second gentleman comes around with a bottle and a glass, some drink, others pour their portion on the ground. I take mine and taste it. It helps intensify the burn the pepper started so I pour the rest on the ground. Then yet another person comes with water in a plastic pitcher and a glass. I pass on the water because it looks gray and there is a small fish in the clear glass pitcher.

After the cola ritual the chief gets up to say, "We the Marylanders in Monrovia have a stranger with us. We have given you the cola to share our energy and we have given you cola for strength and pepper to heal and to cleanse. The water shows the purity of our intentions, and the cane juice shows our willingness to quench your thirst and make you comfortable. Now we ask you, why are you here?" A short round man comes to stand beside the chief and translates what was said into the language of the people.

Alita stands and tells the crowd, "I am not a stranger, Liberia is my home. I was here when Liberia was Liberia. My husband is a son of this soil."

The man with the animal tail stops her and the short man translates her words to the dialect. The elderly people in attendance nod their heads in agreement and all in the audience cheer.

Alita continues, "I have brought with me my mate, to come and celebrate his life and the transition he is making. We come to do the false burial to release him from this life so he may continue his journey through the universe." When she is finished, she sits down.

The short man acts as translator again and makes everyone aware of what was said. Then the man on the short stool stands.

"Daughter, welcome home. Some of our people cross the ocean and break the canoe. You and your husband have made us proud. We welcome you home, we welcome your mate, and we give you safe passage."

Alita stands again to say "We thank you and we thank God."

The interpreter does his job and the crowd claps enthusiastically.

When she sits again, the head of the Marylanders in Monrovia says. "We have prepared a little food for you to eat. Come and allow us to host you in a meal."

I start to get up but Alita looks at me to say, "We will remain seated. They will bring us food."

The women immediately begin serving from a table laden with food. We are quickly given plates with potato salad, fish, and a long white chunk of what Alita tells me is cassava.

"They have prepared what they consider American dishes in your honor," Alita tells me.

"How nice of them." I taste and everything is delicious even if it does have my sweat dripping into it. The mosquitoes are eating me in earnest. It's hard to scratch discreetly when your arms and legs are begging to be cut off. The bumps are becoming as big as grapes and the desire to scratch is similar to the desire to eat after a four day fast. I won't forget the repellant again.

Weah comes back over to where we are sitting. He speaks to Alita after spearing me with a glance. The look leaves no question about how little he thinks of me. The dialect is quick and even if it were slow, it would have been too much for me.

"Weah, No" Alita says before switching to dialect.

After a five minute conversation, Alita tells him, "I will hear no more of this."She turns her face away from him and he could not miss the fact this was the end of the conversation.

He turns to leave which gives me the chance to ask, "What was that all about?"

"Weah thinks you should not go to Maryland. He feels the travel will be too much and you are not aware enough of our culture to effectively participate in the ceremony."

"What did you tell him?"

"I thanked him for his concern and told him you are much stronger than you appear."

"He probably wanted to choke you when you said that. He has got to be the meanest person I've ever met. Sorry for saying so, since he is your relative."

"No, he is not mean. But he needs to understand his aversion to anyone not Liberian is ridiculous."

"He doesn't like me because I'm not Liberian?"

"He doesn't like you because he doesn't know you."

"Well, I'm not jumping over the moon about him either. He is the only person to be excessively rude, except for the airport people."

"Weah is a wonderful person. He just has moments like this on occasion."

"I would hate to be his wife."

"Weah is not married. He was at one time, for twelve years. His wife left him and went to the United States. He never fully forgave her even though it's been twenty years ago."

"It's easy to relate to the hurt he must have felt, but he should probably get over it." If Robert and I don't get back together, I don't want to still be bitter twenty years later.

After everyone is finished eating, the chief gets up to speak. The call to attention works immediately. Shorty the translator comes back to stand beside Alita.

The chief of the Marylanders stands and speaks. "Daughter, you have come home to us. We will send you to your birthplace, the place where your navel string is buried with our protection. Please accept a man to travel with you to ease the path."

"Chief, you honor me and my mate with such a kind gesture."

"Weah," the chief calls.

Weah steps forward quickly and he begins to speak with the chief in dialect. The kind woman sitting beside me begins to fill me in on what I'm missing, and puts to rest my prayers it is not what I think they are discussing.

"The chief has just told Weah he is to accompany you to Maryland. Weah is telling the chief he cannot leave at this time, he is preparing a farm for harvest," the interpreter tells me. "The chief is telling Weah we the Marylanders will harvest his crops. He will honor his people by being the escort."

Damn, damn, damn. Of all the people to have to travel with, we get Mr. Meany.

Weah speaks and the translation is "You put great faith in me. I will not disappoint my people. I am honored."

The look he gives to me says he would be more honored to be drug through Monrovia's streets butt naked with wild dogs snapping at his genitals. A look at Alita shows she has her usual smile in place.

He comes over and tells her something I don't understand before leaving the gathering. We are talking and listening for another hour when Alita tells me, "Weah will let me know what time we will be leaving. It will be the day after tomorrow. It's time for us to go now. We have done our duty here."

She looks to find Weah and waves. She laughs, and then squeezes my hand before telling me, "This should be interesting."

We head home to find Woapla and Wilhelmina waiting up for us. Our clothing has arrived and we take turns trying them on. Alita teaches me how to wrap the lappa and head wrap. I am amazed at how African I look. Afterwards, Alita shoos Wilhelmina and Woapla off to bed. We talk a bit longer before retiring for the night.

My bed feels as comfortable as before, but my body is anything but relaxed. The air is heavy as though it's had an infusion of lead. I can't tell if air has entered my body or if it has exited my body. The air doesn't move enough to shift the position of the cobwebs in the corners of my brain or relieve the pain from the mosquito bites on my appendages. Thankfully, the swelling is beginning to recede. Finally, after what seems like hours, there are familiar fingers closing my eyes against the Liberian moon.

When sunlight invades, I get back up and prowl around the room. About a half hour later, the door opens and Alita enters.

She asks, "Dear one, are you feeling well?"

"Yes, I was just getting acquainted with the place."

"Good. We are invited to meet with the senator. She was here while you were sleeping, and wishes us to join her for supper. She is cooking the meal herself, which is an honor. She has a cook and for her to go into the kitchen to cook is a sign of her regard and esteem towards us. Would you like to attend or shall I send regrets?"

"The senator? Sounds exciting and dinner sounds like a good thing. What should I wear?"

"Be comfortable. We leave in an hour for shopping. There is food in the kitchen if you are hungry. Here, this is for you." Alita comes to place a piece of metal in my hands.

In my hand is a long skeletal looking key. "What is this for?"

"It is for you. If ever you feel the desire to return, this is your home. The key is to this suite."

"There's no way I would come here without you."

"You never know where life will take you. Keep the key as a memento if you believe you will never use it. Keep it as a way to enter if you decide to return."

"Thank you Alita, you are very kind."

"It is not kindness, it is your right. Now, I will leave you to prepare for the day."

My laughter fills the suite. Imagine, me having a key to a place in another country. Again laughter bubbles up and the feeling of freedom is only eclipsed by the heat.

After breakfast, we go back to the area called Waterside. We shop until early afternoon, buying unusual ivory items, carved wooden figures, and leather purses. When we go back home, Woapla has prepared a light snack since we are going out for dinner.

Alita gives me a cell phone and says, "You may want to call your family and tell them you are safely in Liberia."

I go into the bedroom and call Lynette. She answers on the first ring. "Hi Lynette, could you let everyone know I'm here in Liberia and I love them"

"Mom, I'm glad you called. How is everything?"

"It's wonderful. I am having a great time."

"Daddy said if you called to tell you…"

"Sorry Lynette, you're breaking up. I'll call back soon." I am not about to allow Robert to tell me anything. I know there is nothing positive he has to say.

An hour later Alita comes into the private sitting room dressed in mauve flowered fabric with sandals on her feet. "Can you be ready to leave in twenty minutes?"

"Yes. Will this dress do for the occasion?" I hold up a green tie die dress and sandals that will allow my feet to breathe in the heat.

"You will look lovely."

I dress and my exposed areas are bathed in mosquito repellant. We head out as the sky is changing to a lovely shade of bluish pink. Joseph has the car at the front and hurriedly opens the doors for us to enter. After a short drive, we pull in front of a two-story brick house. The porch covers the entire front of the property and there are trees in the front yard.

A short round older woman comes out to meet us attired in a stylish colorful long skirt, a matching top with puffy sleeves, and a matching headdress kisses Alita on both cheeks. Then she turns to me. She embraces me in a hug and introduces herself.

"I am Senator Beatrice Tambla, from Maryland County. Welcome home."

"It is a pleasure to meet you, thank you for inviting me to dinner. I'm not actually from here. I just came with Alita."

"You are African American, is that correct?"

"Yes."

"Do you know from what part of Africa you ancestors came?"

"No."

"Then it could have well been Liberia, so welcome home. You may call me Cousin Bea." She then takes my hand and leads me into her home.

Alita follows us into a spacious sunken living room. The blue tile on the floor has curious designs in red and yellow. The walls have large windows to allow the outside into the space and create a feeling of energy. We sit on the various carved wooden seats with plump cushions she has in groups around the room.

"Tirana, please bring refreshments for our guests."

A young lady appears bearing a pitcher with tall golden glasses. She pours an amber colored beverage into each glass and passes one to each of us.

"Iced tea is ready. There is also beer or wine if you would care for something different." Cousin Bea offers.

"Iced tea is fine." My glass is cold and the taste is sweet, cooling and welcome in the heat.

Cousin Bea and Alita talk briefly about the state of Liberian politics. My contribution to the conversation is limited. This is not a topic I ever thought I would have a need to discuss. My ears perk up a bit later when I hear what they are talking about.

"Alita you must return and contribute to your country," Cousin Bea states.

"My contribution to my country is to support candidates like you, who have a genuine caring for the people and who will not allow the corruption that plagues so many African countries to become systemic to this region.

"You would surely win any office you desire," Cousin Bea persists.

"As I told you earlier, I have no desire to win an office. I have a full and meaningful life already. Lynn and I have been shopping and have barely had a bite to eat."

The broad hint to change the subject causes Cousin Bea to smile and say, "I am sure you are trying to change the subject, so for now, come."

We go up the three stairs to the dining room. Dishes are sitting on the table and after a prayer of thanksgiving Cousin Bea starts the meal by passing around a salad followed by cornbread. There is red wine with short red glasses around the bottle and the beer is on ice. I opt for the cold of the beer. The dinner conversation is a continuation of politics and the history of the country.

Bea continues my lesson on Liberia. "The Americo Liberians brought a system of taxation. They would go from one village to another to collect taxes. However, the villages had no car road. Therefore, when the tax collectors were ready to go they would take all of their family along. Sometimes there were eight to ten people in the family, with the tax collector, each wife and each child in their own hammock. The native people were required to tote the family from one village to another to collect money from the chiefs."

"While in one village, they would send to the next village to let them know how many people they would need to carry everyone. Sometimes they would need seventy-five people to one hundred people to tote the load. The village would be on standby to carry the tax collectors and their family from one village to the next. The tax collectors would not want to get down from the perch, thinking themselves above staying overnight in any one village or even setting their foot on the soil. Women would be required to tote the load if not enough men were there to carry the people. The only exception for carrying a load was if you were going to school or going to church. Then, you could not tote a load," Cousin Bea explains.

"It seems horrible for a government to behave in such a manner. I can't imagine what it would be like to have to carry another human," I tell her. "How were the taxes assessed?"

"The taxes were five to seven dollars per house. They would collect all the taxes and bring it to the capital city, all the while neglecting any development in the villages. The money was supposed to improve the capital city of each county with the remainder sent to the federal government. Many people believe the Americo Liberians used the money to educate their children. Even now the lack of development in the rural areas is deplorable," Alita shares.

"It makes our tax system look great. We have the money taken out before we even get it."

"It sounds like a superior system. Here is the beginning of our main course," Cousin Bea says as she passes around a bowl of rice.

We all take a serving. Rice would not be my ideal main course, but when in Liberia, do as the Liberians. I mimic Alita in preparing my plate and have a mound of rice then make a valley in the middle.

"Remember the pioneer children used to say, 'The love of liberty brought us here'," Alita shares.

"They forget liberty met them here'." the Senator interjects. "It is the time now for the country to work for all the people and not just a certain group. That is why we need our people to return," she says with a look and a smile at Alita.

She picks up another bowl and dishes the contents on top of the rice before passing it around. Alita takes some and passes the bowl to me. I pile the contents, which are reddish-brown chunks and onions in a pungent smelling sauce, into the valley of rice.

"Let me tell you about the villages where we will be going," Alita steers the conversation. "There are four villages, Fishtown, Rocktown, Cavalla, and Middletown, which is our destination. Each is divided between those who go to church and those who do not go to church. You must cross the 'sada' or rock wave to the other side where the Christians live. Rocktown, Cavalla, and Fishtown are all divided the same way."

"Rocktown is the home of the largest rocks along the coast. You can climb up onto the mountains and look over the ocean. You will not be able to take pictures there because there is a spirit in the rocks that protects the area from the sea," Alita tells me.

"This will be an adventure. Little old me from Wichita, Kansas having an adventure like Dorothy from the Wiz." I grab a spoon of food from my dish and midway to my mouth, curiosity causes me to ask, "What is this? It looks and smells delicious." I bring the contents close to my mouth while I wait for the answer.

"Bar-b-cue snail," Cousin Bea informs me and puts a mouthful into her mouth.

Alita seems to be enjoying hers immensely judging by the look of bliss on her face. Kiss my ass. Damn, I'm going to have to eat this. I direct my spoon of snail, onions, bar-b-cue sauce and rice into my mouth. After only a small hesitation, I push it in.

The only thing worse than having snails prepared in bar-b-cue sauce and onions served over rice go down your throat is the sensation of having them crawl out of the bed of salad and cornbread to make their way slowly back up your throat. I grab the beer bottle and down half of it in a single gulp. I finish the beer when it registers that the bar-b-cue sauce must have been made in habanera peppers hell and my tongue is on fire.

Great. I have snails swimming in a beer pool and trying to climb out of my throat, which is now covered with third degree burns. My eyes are watering and I can't seem to get anyone to notice there is going to be a really bad thing happening soon. I'm sure Liberian senators are as averse as American senators are to having dead bodies in their home with bar-b-cued snails coming out of their nose.

Finally, Alita looks at me. "Are you alright? You are sweating profusely."

"Hot, hot" I manage to squeak out past my scorched lips.

Cousin Bea reaches one side at about the same time Alita reaches the other.

"Oh the pepper. I wasn't thinking you might not be able to eat pepper. Sorry, sorry, sorry," Cousin Bea says clucking like a hen. She calls out, "Tirana. Bring milk. Our stranger can't eat pepper. Come quickly!"

Alita takes her hand and wipes the sweat from my brow and the tears from my eyes. I wipe my nose and am surprised to see there are no snails coming out of the nostrils. Tirana comes running with a bottle of milk while I try to hang on to life and stop the tears from running down my face and the snot running down my nose. When the tears touch my burning lips, the pain gets worse because of their saltiness.

"Water, please water."

"Not water. Water would make it burn worse. The milk will cool and soothe you." Alita assures me and pushes the glass towards me as she fans me with a magazine.

I gulp the milk and feel a measure immediate relief. The milk also soothes the snails enough there is no longer a fear we would be seeing them again coming back the same throat they went down. Now the imminent danger is past, the sense of shame creeps in.

"That was a little unexpected. I'm so sorry. Please finish eating." My voice is raspy and pitched low so as not to hurt too badly. I would rather starve than eat another bite of anything, but I'm sure they are hungry and used to the burn.

"Lynn, maybe it is time for us to leave," Alita says.

"No, no, please let's not leave. We're having great conversation. It was unexpected to find the food so, so, spicy. I'll have some more rice. It would be silly to leave." My shame would be enormously more profound if we leave because of my inability to eat what they are having.

Alita touches my shoulder. "Remember what I told you in Cannes. There is no shame in refusing what is offered."

"Yes, yes, but I do want to stay. I'll just be more careful with tasting new foods."

Alita is convinced after I squeeze her hand and tell her, "Let me make this decision please."

Cousin Bea clucks a bit longer before they sit back down. They resume their spicy meal as my bland rice soothes the snails in my stomach. The conversation starts again and I learn even more about Liberia. After dinner, we go into the living room and talk about the plans for the false burial. Finally, it is time to go home.

"Is there anything you are allergic to or don't like?" Alita asks as we are heading back home. "I didn't think about dietary restrictions."

"I don't really care for cats."

"Cats cooked or cats alive?"

Oh shit, I may be losing some weight while I'm here is my thought before her smile lightens my concern.

"Relax and enjoy," she tells me as she reaches out to squeeze my arm.

We make it back to the house and as we pull into the driveway, I comment on something about the house that had been haunting me. "Alita, this home is so very similar to the one in Paris."

"Yes, the furnishings are different otherwise they are almost the same house."

"Why? I mean you have the house already in France, why recreate it?"

"We liked the style. When we purchased the home in Paris, we replicated it here. He designed the home and spent time here to make sure it was built according to his specifications."

"There is so much about him I didn't know."

"You had a short time together. Why did you always refuse to see him again?" Alita's question catches me off guard.

As we enter the house, I answer her. "I didn't want the inevitable pain."

"Why inevitable?"

"It would have been difficult. I was married, he was married. I always felt that if we continued to see each other, I would want more of him or he would want less of me. Looking back on it, the reasons seem weak. I miss him."

"As do I. It is right we will bury him together. Come, it is time to rest."

When we get to the house, Woapla is waiting up for me. "Auntie Lynn, Boku Weah told me to pack your things so you will be ready to leave. He said you would not be able to get them ready in time. I have left out your night clothes and Boku chose something for you to wear tomorrow. Your things are in the corner." She gestures to my meager belongings.

My choice of traveling attire would have been the tie dye dress Weah had selected, but it reminded me too much of Robert's dictatorship for me to allow his selection of my clothing to pass unchallenged.

"How dare he pick what I'm going to wear? He can't tell me what to wear." I look at Alita. "Don't you think he is overstepping?"

Alita shrugs.

"Woapla, take my things back in the room. I am old enough to dress myself and can certainly pick out what I want to wear tomorrow."

Woapla looks at Alita who shrugs yet again and then takes my luggage back in the room. I select a cotton blouse designed to show off my twins and a flared skirt to wear and smile smugly while I put the other clothing back into the suitcase and drag it to the corner of the front room where it came from. Satisfied with my efforts, I climb into bed and fight the heat.

I NOW CHRISTEN YOU THE RUSTY BUCKET

Wednesday morning, Alita enters my room. "Come Lynn, Weah will arrive soon to take us to the port. We will spend the night on the water."

It is bright daylight outside and her words dash any hope Weah taking us to Maryland was a dream or rather a nightmare. "Does he really have to go with us? He's like a dark cloud waiting to rain on my parade."

"It is a question of honor now. He is responsible for getting us there and back safely. Lynn, you do not have to talk with him."

"It's hard not to feel his disapproval." Besides, I can't speak enough dialect to talk to him.

"Think of this as an adventure. Now come, Cherie. He is probably waiting for us."

Sure enough Weah is in the front room. Woapla and Wilhelmina are bustling around packing food for us. We go and have breakfast as they leave for school. Weah looks at my attire and says something to Alita she doesn't bother to translate. I give him a broad smile.

He wrinkles his nose and his eyes become slits in his face as he gives a parody of a smile. Weah barks out something else and heads towards the door. Alita follows him so I follow her. We get to the car and instead of allowing Joseph to drive; Weah gets into the driver's seat. Joseph is relegated to passenger status.

It doesn't take long to arrive at the port and when we exit, I look around hoping to see the ship we are to take to Cape Palmas.

Weah makes a grunt and speaks to Alita.

She turns to me to say, "Our ship is right here."

When I think of a ship, my point of reference was the Nautica Queen, a ship for passengers to go on a cruise of Lake Erie. It was a journey taken with Mr. M.O.P. years ago in Cleveland. This ship is rust held together by paint, nails, and hemp rope. Seaworthy is not a phrase even remotely associated with this floating hulk of rusted metal.

"Alita, do you think this is safe?"

Weah turns to look at me. I turn my body pointedly to look at Alita.

Again she gives her African European shrug. "We shall see."

Weah says something and heads away from us. There is a small commotion as we board the wooden ramp. It is easy to misstep into the gaps in the gangplank where wood is missing, so concentration is required. If I had to carry anything, it would have been a repeat of the incident at the airport. At the top of the ramp as I step onto the ship the feeling of climbing Mount Everest is present in my heart.

The commotion continues as we stand and look around. A short squat man rushes forward to say "You are most welcome to my ship, Mrs. Alita." He grabs Alita's arm to kiss her hand and shake it at the same time.

His eyes never travel more than breast high and if he opens his mouth and stands closer, one of her tits would go right in.

"Captain thank you for your kindness in granting us passage. We are happy your ship is going to Cape Palmas. Allow me to introduce Lynn Westner," she says as she turns to get his mouth away from her personal space.

"When Weah told me of your need to reach Maryland, how could I not be at your service?" He turns to me and stops in the middle of his welcome. His eyes are on the enhancement of my breasts.

The captain continues to glue his eyes on my ta tas. "Such a pleasure, such a pleasure." He rubs his pudgy little hands together and flexes his fingers in the air in front of him, palms out.

"Nice to meet you, sir."

"Sir? Nonsense, I am Kwame. Please let me show you my ship, Miss. Lynn. Mrs. Alita, I will ensure her arrival at her cabin. I have the VI.P. suites for you and her. They are adjoining. I would so enjoy having the opportunity to show her around." Again the flexing, as if he is squeezing my melons.

Alita looks questioningly towards me.

"I would love to see your ship captain." He's short enough for me not to be afraid he might try something, if he does, I'll pound him in the top of his head.

Alita tells me, "Enjoy your tour Lynn," then gives me a wink and follows a young man in jeans and a sailor cap toward the far side of the ship.

"Please lead the way captain." I'll do anything to make my time on the Rusty Bucket go faster.

There is a push from behind me and I am propelled, titties first, into the good captain. His little hands doing their flex action, now slightly cover my breasts. The cause of the push is Weah not watching where he is going. Weah quickly gets my body away from the captain by putting his arm around my waist and pulling me body back towards him. My back is attached to Weah's front with the captain's hands still on my boobs. Lord, not another threesome.

"Excuse me, captain." The look I give to Weah over my shoulder would have scorched a normal man. Weah benignly drops his arm from my waist and walks in front of me and toward the captain. The captain walks backward as Weah walks forward. When they are a few feet away, Weah speaks to him in the dialect. Weah glances back once in my direction and taps the side of his head with his index finger.

The captain takes his eyes from my titties and looks me in the face. The heat from the day is causing sweat on his brow, "Oh. Sorry, sorry. I'm sure you're exhausted" he tells me.

"I'm not the least bit tired."

"Oh sure you are, sure you are." he tells me. "We can see the ship any old time. Yes, yes, any old time." Captain looks at Weah again wipes his brow with the back of his hand. He grabs the sailor who is passing and hurries off to parts unknown. "Poor thing, she's not quite right in the head," I hear him saying.

I turn around to Weah, "Is he talking about me? What did you tell him? Damn, I wish someone could tell me what you said to him."

Weah scowls at me, picks up my bags and with a head jerk motions me to follow him.

I just know he is the reason I am not getting a tour of the ship. I childishly stick my tongue out at his retreating form. "You sure are a mean bastard even if you are eye candy," I tell his back, glad he doesn't know what I'm saying.

He stops and turns but there is no one here to interpret my words. I give him my most innocent smile until he turns and starts moving again. He doesn't stop moving until we are at the door of my room.

I look at him and smile while telling him, "If you weren't so easy on the eye, I would kick you in your left leg for the fun of it, you jerk. And I hope you like my clothes, as you can see I am able to dress myself. How do you like that Mr. Grumpy Ass?" I reach out and touch his arm. He jumps as if I had put acid on him. Again I keep the smile in place and keep looking into his eyes. The smile must have thrown him because he almost smiles back, no doubt thinking he is receiving a compliment.

He opens the door to my room and drops my luggage just inside the door on the floor and turns to leave the room. His exit gives me the opportunity to examine my space. The VIP suite has a wooden sleeping area under the round window that opens to the outside almost two feet above. The bed is six feet long and covers the entire bottom of the wall. There is a bathroom I hope I don't have to use. The inside of the commode is black even though it is a white standard toilet. Note to self; don't drink anything until we reach land.

I climb on my sleeping space and stand to look out of the portal and reflect on how I came to be in this place. Everything since my arrival in France has been an adventure. The episode with Alita brings warmth to private places. After half an hour, it appears we are finally leaving and heading out the port to our destination.

Watching the waves roll and roll and roll make my stomach roll and roll and roll. I sink down on the hard wood bed/seat and lay down even though I'm not tired. There is a loud insect buzzing in my ears preventing me from going to sleep. It must be a fly and it seems murder must be committed if I am to get any rest. My brain looks for and discards weapons to kill the intruder. I think about the magazine stuffed into my bag.

I stumble up to transform my magazine into a fly swatter. With weapon in hand I go back to the bed to search for the pest. I can't find it on the wall and stand perfectly still to catch the sound again. The rumbling tone comes from under the pillow. I snatch the pillow out of the way and with my hand wrapped around the rolled up magazine and my arm in the air ready to strike, prepare to give the fly a date with destiny.

Instead of finding a fly, I am confronted with a very large, very angry, and very loud bug the size of a mouse. It moves quickly the way creepy crawly things move, and leaves the bed to crawl onto the floor and head in my direction. My scream brings Weah into the room before all of the sound could escape my mouth. My shaking pointing finger shows him the dragon he has been summoned to slay on the floor waiting to kill me.

He lifts his substantial foot and brings it down on the unidentified bug beast. The sound of what I believe is bone breaking is audible in the confines of the room.

"What the fuck? You just stepped on that thing. Now what?"

He lifts his foot to show me the bloody carcass.

The excitement of finding the live attacking thing become a squashed lump of red and black mixes with the motion of the ocean. Weah looks in my face. He senses what is coming next just before I give him the remainder of my breakfast, still warm from my stomach, from his waist to his shoes.

The shock on his face is the last thing I see before spots in my vision let me know there will soon be one more creature on the floor. My body crumbles and I feel his arms around me just before I hit the jumbled mess he has created. I hear his bellow for Alita since he calls her name loud and long and the sound rumbles through his chest where my face now resides. I feel him carry me toward the bed and hear the door open before the faint is complete.

When I have my next conscious thought, I am in the bed with a sheet covering my naked body. Alita is beside me and takes the cloth off my head. She dips it into a pan of water and places it back onto my forehead. My mouth tastes awful and my throat is sore.

"Alita I think your cousin hates me."

"Ridiculous. Of course he doesn't hate you, he doesn't know you."

"I think he hates me because I threw up on him."

Alita gives me a glass and holds out a large plastic bowl. "Rinse your mouth and spit. I'm sure your throwing up was not intentional. Weah knows that. How are you feeling?"

"Aside from my pride taking a severe beating, I feel weak"

"Not to worry, you will be fine. Just a little mal de mer."

"What is that? I still feel woozy," I tell her.

"You call it sea sickness," Alita tells me as she fiddles with the sheet covering me.

"I hope I get better soon."

"You will be fine."

"What about the thing on my bed Weah killed?"

"A roach."

"A roach? It was as big as my hand." I think of the little cockroaches in Wichita and give thanks.

"Yes, dear one, we have rather large roaches in Africa."

"It had to be at least five inches."

"Yes, well, Weah cleaned it up. It won't harm you, but it is loud. I have checked the room and have not found any more," she tells me.

I think about my state of undress. "Did you take my clothes off, Alita?" I hope so. She's seen me naked on more than one occasion.

"No, I did not. Actually Weah took your soiled clothes off of you. He was most insistent."

"He saw me naked. Oh no."

"He saw you naked, oh yes. When I entered, you were in his arms and unconscious. Weah told me to go get water to clean you. Once I came back with the water, you were in bed naked. I tried to tell him I would clean you, but he insisted. He mentioned it was his fault you became ill. He felt the responsibility to get you do all he could to make you comfortable. I was present as he did so. He was very attentive and interested."

"He's so mean to me and I know he hates me, now."

"I would beg to differ on your assessment. But for now rest and regain your strength. We arrive in Cape Palmas in the morning." Alita kisses me on the cheek, tucks in the sheet again. She refreshes the cloth in the water and puts it on my forehead. The scent of lemons helps my eyes to close.

When I wake again, Weah is in the room sitting on the end of the bed watching me. I feel almost brand new aside from being hungry and having a slight headache.

"Hello Mr. Grumpy. I sure could use something to eat. I'm starving. I promise to try to keep it down this time if you don't kill any bugs in my presence. I wish you could at least talk to me."

Weah stares at me with no expression at all.

"If I want anything, I'll need to get it myself. Lack of communication is a bitch." I start to sit up and remember I have no clothes on. I pull the sheet further up to my chin and lie back down.

He gives me a hard look before holding out the tie dyed dress he had suggested I wear in the first place. I snatch it out of his hands and he stands. He looks hard at me again and I can see a hint of concern in his eyes. Probably because it is now his responsibility to make sure I return to Monrovia in pretty much the same condition I was in when I left.

He turns to walk toward the door. At the door he tells me, "Ah me nee oh."

Alita soon enters with a bowl of clear soup. "Hello Lynn, Weah said you may be hungry. This should take off the edge of hunger without upsetting your stomach."

I welcome the soup and then test my sea legs. When I stand, I don't fall over, but I do still feel dizzy. Alita takes my dress and helps me put it on. I look out of the window for a few minutes, and then I get back into the bed. I rest some more while Alita describes the coastline we are passing.

"If you could look out at the outgrowth of trees on the huge peak there you would have your first glimpse of Cape Palmas."

I take a quick look out of the window. It shows it is very different from the trees in Sedona, with the red dirt and red rocks. Here there is a green lushness. The palm trees remind me of a hand waving, welcoming us to the area. We get closer and closer until we round the trees and head into port.

"Alita it's beautiful. How could you leave here?"

A sound alerts us to Weah as he comes in and looks at me. He says something to Alita and heads back out.

She says to me, "Come, we can go upstairs and prepare to disembark. Weah will ensure our luggage follows."

There is a crowd of people at the port. The gangplank is set and we are soon allowed off the floating hazard. I had doubts about the safety of the ship and look at Alita, happy we were successful in our journey. Weah is at the rear of us and takes over to get us bundled into a waiting car.

CHICKEN GIFTS, DUCK BATHS AND A FALSE BURIAL

We head into Harper, the capital of Maryland County. There is a SUV waiting for us and Weah gets us settled in with our luggage. The driver takes us down paved streets with large concrete homes. Alita points out other points of interest as we drive away.

"There is the home of President Tubman. He was the longest serving president in Liberia. He served for over forty years and he was from Maryland County. The home has an entrance from the sea because the president was an avid boater."

The three story mansion could have easily fit into estates in California. She also points out the library and Tubman University. We eventually stop in front of a mint green building.

"Lynn, we will be spending the night here for a ceremony similar to the one in Monrovia. You may want to prepare yourself for a long evening. Tomorrow we will go to Middletown for the false burial."

We enter the home. It is lovely with tile floors and bright paint on the walls. I am greeted by a round woman named Gladys. She has a raspy voice that makes her accent even more pronounced.

She hugs me close and tells me, "Thank you, thank you. I will be taking care of you. I will go with you to the village and serve as your interpreter. Let me show you to your room." Gladys heads down a hallway and I have no choice but to follow. "I will take something out for you to wear and meet the people tonight. If there is anything you need you call me."

"Thank you Gladys. I'm Lynn and I'm planning on wearing my salmon outfit to the meeting. I love this place already. It's sunny and green and I feel great being on land after the ship ride."

"Sorry, sorry, the ride down was not good. I'll get you some water. You want to drink plenty water so you don't get dehydrated."

The bed is low to the floor and looks comfortable. The closet is open and the windows take up almost half of the walls. The cross breeze is appreciated and I sit in a chair to relax.

"You have two hours until the meeting," Gladys tells me when she comes back in with a bottle of water.

"I'll be ready. Do you know where I can find Alita?"

"She is resting. She asked me to tell you she will see you before the meeting."

I look out at the trees and other activity visible from my bedroom until it is time to get dressed. I pick up the outfit from the bed and Gladys comes back to help ensure my attire is correct.

Alita and Weah are in the living room. "Hello Alita." I make the appropriate noise to Weah and sit down.

"Cherie, we will soon leave for the meeting. It will thankfully be short and sweet since all know we leave tomorrow for the false

178

burial. Weah was just telling me we will go to Middletown by road. He wants us to be ready early, at least by eight o'clock."

"No problem. I'll be ready."

Weah stands up and heads towards the door. He looks at me and I remain seated. He turns to Alita and speaks rapidly before leaving the room.

"Let's go," Alita tells me.

"He said a lot of words for it's time to go. Was there anything else?"

"The important part was it is time for us to leave," Alita laughs.

Weah drives us a short distance to another home. We get out and experience the same ceremony we had in Monrovia. The cola is still bitter and the pepper is still hot. I pour the cane juice in his memory and allow Gladys to tell me everything everyone is saying.

Alita is obviously tired when we get back. She is not moving as fast as normal and I ask her, "Alita, are you going to be okay? You seem, I don't know, as if you are wilting."

"The ceremonies are draining. Being back here is not burdensome, but it is a reminder he is not off on a gig, he is gone and I miss him."

I walk over to hug her. Inside the hug we have the opportunity to remember him. Our shared sorrow is unique, because if he were alive, I would not be here, and would likely have never seen her again. We hold each other, allow our tears to mingle, and share comfort from the embrace of the other. We don't need words, just a person to hold onto for a while.

"Thank you Lynn. It is good to have your understanding."

"I'm glad you invited me."

"It grows late. We will talk more tomorrow." She gives me a final hug before going to bed.

Friday morning bright and early, Gladys comes to wake me up. I choose to travel in my salmon lappa suit since there will be a meeting as soon as we arrive. Once we are all in the jeep-type car, we head out with Weah driving. The vehicle has a second rear seat where our luggage and Gladys reside.

After driving for more twenty minutes, we make a hard left turn into the bushes. Weah continues to drive and it strikes me there is no road. We are driving through tall grass. Gladys is snoring lightly from beside me and attempting conversation with Weah would be pointless since I already know his name.

"How does he know where he is going," I ask Alita.

Weah turns to throw a haughty glance at me.

"He is very familiar with the road to Middletown. We have traveled this path many times before," Alita assures me.

"But there isn't a road. There's nothing but bushy grass."

"The Savannah grass is plentiful here. If you look closely, Lynn, you will see the road. We used to walk this road when we were younger. There is also a way to get to Middletown by going along the seacoast," Alita explains.

I look closer out of the windshield, and sure enough there is a footpath where you can see dirt. It is about three feet wide and if you move too much on either side, you would step off of the path into the grass.

After another hour I tell Alita, "This constant rocking is hard on my bladder."

She and Weah have a short conversation before she tells me, "We will pull over when there is another clearing so we can relieve ourselves."

Sure enough after another twenty minutes, he pulls over. Clearing is relative. There is still Savannah grass on all four sides. This will obviously be an outdoor experience in bladder release, something I cannot ever remember doing.

Alita passes me some tissue and tells me, "You may need this."

Gladys wakes up long enough to climb out and head to a space in the grass, well hidden. Alita does the same in a different direction and I strike out in yet another direction.

I squat down and proceed to relieve myself. Surprisingly a lappa skirt is also a hindrance. The skirt has to be held up by one hand and the other hand has to be held in front of me to give me balance. My legs have to be spread far enough apart that my ankles and the back of my legs don't get wet, but short of taking my panties all of the way off, it was a tight squeeze.

There is a sound from behind me. The sound from the bushes gets closer causing my urine flow to stop mid stream. Having my panties close to my ankles is going to make it difficult to run but whatever is in these bushes seems big enough to cause serious trouble. Seconds after my panties reach my ass a large blur comes through the bushes. The scream coming loud and fast past my lips is a signal to my feet to move quickly. The group gathered by the car looks up at my approach, lappa skirt still in my hand, pulled up around my waist. Weah grabs me first and stops my flight by putting his arm around my waist.

Alita asks me, "What is it Lynn?"

"In the bushes, something is in the bushes."

Weah rushes to the area recently evacuated by me. A few minutes later he comes back with a frown creasing the skin between his eyes and his lips turned downward. He rolls his eyes at me before saying something I don't understand to Alita.

Alita starts laughing then tells me, "Lynn, were you running from a pig in the bushes?"

"I don't know what I was running from. It was a pig! Why the hell is there a pig in the bushes? Don't people keep their damn pigs locked up in a pigpen? Why are pigs running loose terrorizing innocent people?"

Another sound comes from the bushes and the cause of my still not empty bladder saunters over to root around the tires of the car. No one except me finds this unusual. The pig doesn't even look my way after having seen my holes exposed earlier. When it finds nothing edible, it moves away, back into the bushes.

Weah gets into the car. Alita and Gladys hug me.

"Sorry, sorry," Gladys clucks.

"Lynn, there is much that is different here, but nothing to harm you," Alita tells me as she guides me back to the bushes so I can completely empty my bladder.

Our arrival in Middletown is met by cheers. As the car parks on the outside of a semi-circle of one story homes, there are children jumping and laughing. In the middle of the semi-circle, there are chairs set as they were in Monrovia and Harper for the welcome ceremony.

This time, after the introductions and the sharing of the cola, Alita stands. She goes over to a small circle of fire burning next to a green home. The fire pit has long sticks surrounding it and is about eighteen inches in diameter. She starts talking in her dialect and Gladys interprets.

"I call on the spirit of my ancestors, those who have gone before, my mother, my father, my grandmother, my grandfather, my brothers and sisters, my aunts and uncles, my cousins and those who raised me. I am your daughter and I have come home. I have come here to our fire hot. I have come to the place where my navel string is buried. I come to bury my husband, your son. And I cry tears for him."

When she finishes speaking, she pours cane juice into the fire and flame shoots up over her head. She slowly comes back and takes her seat. Tears are falling freely from her eyes and we hug each other. There are tears on my cheeks and the sorrow is lighter because it is shared.

The chief tells us, "You are welcome here, this is your home. We the people of Middletown will bury our son tomorrow. Tonight we will have the war dance. Now let us eat."

His words are a signal to the women to begin serving. I take rice and fish but do not feel like eating. Soon Gladys takes me to a home and shows me where I will be sleeping. It is a small whitewashed place with four rooms. The front room is eight feet by eight feet front room with a wooden couch and wooden chairs, a dining room with a large table, and three bedrooms. All of the rooms have concrete floors.

"Why is the one room so small," I ask Gladys.

"There is very little time spent indoors. Once the meals are eaten, everything occurs outside. When people visit, they visit outside. There is no need to be indoors."

"Is there a bathroom?"

"There is an outhouse for the village and a bath outside."

She takes me into a bedroom where my overnight bag rests. "You will sleep here. The war dance will be tonight, in about one hour and the women will dance tomorrow morning. Then we will have the false burial."

"Gladys, were you here for the actual burial?"

"Of course, this is my village. I had to come."

"What was it like, an African burial?"

"During the actual burial, in the morning, there was the ringing of the bells. From the time of the first bell until four o'clock, you could not eat anything such as food or water and nothing could be toted on your head."

"When is the time of the first bell?"

"The first bell is nine o'clock. The second bell is nine thirty and the third final bell is ten o'clock

"That was the time for the crying. We cried in the morning, at lunch, and in the evening, visitors didn't laugh, all was sadness for one month, and then we buried him in the family plot. After the burial, the immediate family wore black for the years of mourning. The false burial is a celebration. All you have to do is sit. People will come to you and share stories."

"Thank you for telling me."

Gladys bustles out and a few minutes later, Alita comes to the door with a slim short woman in a lappa suit and head wrap.

"Lynn, this is our mate, Comfort."

Comfort looks at me. The sorrow in her eyes leave no doubt she is still in mourning. I go over and hug her. She returns the gesture. I tell her, "I am so sorry for your loss."

"Comfort doesn't speak English. I will give her your regards and say all that is proper." Alita turns to Comfort and has a conversation. They both look at me.

Alita interprets, "Comfort says our husband chose well. She is glad you have come for the ceremony."

Comfort comes and hugs me again then leaves. Alita follows. I am left to ponder my connection to a woman in a remote village in Africa and prepare for the war dance.

Alita comes to retrieve me when there is a horn blowing. I refresh my mosquito spray. We go outside and into an area with chairs in a circular patter with spaces to allow entrance to the center. Alita sits in the first chair in line; Comfort sits in the second chair and Alita motions for me to sit in the third. Weah is not in sight. Gladys sits beside me and interprets the words of the people that come to talk to me.

Directly across from our seats are a series of logs with hollowed spaces carved in the middle. Two of the logs are over four feet long. There are hand drums and tall drums that reach the chest of the drummer. They are playing and coaxing sounds from the various drums.

The middle of the space is empty except for the ground. Suddenly the drums start a loud steady beat. From the left of our chairs come an army of forty men with leopard heads and animal skin covering their faces and various parts of their body. Their chests are marked with white and red coloring and they all have weapons.

Some men have cutlasses as long as their arms, others have bows and arrows, still others carry short knives and few have with cudgels. They move threateningly through the chairs, keeping time to the beat of the drums. They are waving the weapons perilously close to people, but no one appears to be afraid except for me. Every time one gets close, my eyes close and my head goes down. It seems a strange ending for a woman from Wichita, Kansas to meet her death in a remote village in Liberia.

Gladys speaks from beside me. "The war dance is to celebrate the fact your husband was a hero. The men dress in animal skin because it takes a warrior to kill a leopard or any of the mighty animals represented here. The color on the chest is meant to symbolize purity and blood. Only a pure warrior could kill and provide food for the village. The weapons represent the ability to meet the challenge and defeat the enemy.

The dancers come closer again and show their skill. Gladys says, "They do not make mistakes; they are one with their weapon and can command it to do harm or to be merciful. You cannot identify any of the dancers because this war dance is to honor the warrior that has gone from them. By not showing their individual faces, they are all him."

With this knowledge, it is much easier to appreciate the skill and enjoy the honor and esteem in which the man I met on a plane is held. The dancers continue unabated for hours. How they are able to stay on their feet and not fall down flat from sheer exhaustion is amazing. They run through the village, always coming back to the center.

For three hours the dancers show their respect before running from the area as the drumming stops. Their leaving signals the women sitting in the chairs to prepare the food and drink. By the time the tables are set, the men are back. Weah is among them. I couldn't identify him in the crowd of dancers, and it is jarring I was looking for him. The men are still shirtless but have put on pants. They have left their animal skin and weapons who knows where. When dinner is over it is Alita who stands and addresses the crowd.

"Thank you all for your efforts on behalf of our husband. We thank God and we thank you people. My mates and I are most proud. Now we must prepare for tomorrow."

After the interpreter speaks the dialect, Alita motions for Comfort and me to stand. People come to hug us and tell us goodnight.

The next morning I wake up to Gladys talking to me from the doorway.

"Mo ye. Du pla."

Her lips are moving and something foreign is coming out. What the hell am I supposed to say to get her to speak English or shut up? "I can't get you clear."

She immediately switches to English.

"Are you ready to get up and take a bath?"

"A bath sounds perfect. Let me get my things."

I gather my soap and clothing for the day, the black outfit that promises to keep me hot as the fourth level of hell, and some underwear.

"Where's the tub?"

She looks at me and smiles.

"Follow me."

She goes out the door and stops to pick up two plastic buckets of water. One is steaming, which is a feat in this heat. She heads down a path in the rear of the house for about forty feet until we reach what looks like woven plastic sheets hanging between trees. The writing on them let me know they are rice bags.

She lifts one flap and says, "Your bath."

I go in to an area twelve by twelve feet. It is a plastic rice bag shower that I can see over the top and under the bottom of. There are two large rocks next to each other in the sandy space with a stool off to the side of the rocks. Gladys comes in behind me and sits the two buckets on the rock furthest from the stool.

"Ma'am, you can put your things on the seat. I will put drops in to clean the water. You have your hot water and cold water to mix, one to wash, the other to rinse. You will stand on the rock to wash so your feet will stay clean. I have soft shoes for you to wear back to the house. When you finish, call out for me. Leave the buckets and your nightclothes. I will gather them to wash."

Okay. I knew I wasn't coming to the Ritz, but this is not a bath. It's a wash up. Outdoors. In a plastic rice bag room. I can do this. The most anyone can see is my calves down and my neck up. I put my clothing and toiletries down to mix my water to the correct temperature.

Once the water is just right, I start washing. The water runs down and away from the rock to fill up the small spaces in the ground. I cannot remember ever being outside naked in my life. Being outside in Africa naked makes me want to sing to myself because I feel free. I make up a song about washing the various parts of my body. I sing to please myself since no one else is here. Or so I thought.

My head is tilted back as I'm singing about washing my arms. Then I hear an unusual sound, like a duck quacking. The song gets stuck in my throat as my eyes fly open to see what the hell is going on. While I am doing my Aretha Franklin imitation, a group of five little ducks had marched into my bathroom. Six counting the runt just coming through the bottom of my wall.

"Hey get out of here. I'm taking a bath."

They continue to march determinedly towards me on my rock perch.

"Shoo. Get out."

Not only did they not get out, their mother comes in. She is big and unfriendly judging from the glare in the beady eye she is staring at me with. She turns and looks at her children then turns both beady eyes my way and starts toward me. Hell, I didn't do anything to them, they invaded my space. At this point, I can try to defend myself or run naked back to the house. Damn. I'm not running.

"GET OUT!"

The little ones pay me not a bit of attention. The mother obviously does not appreciate being told what to do and starts a hell of a loud noise.

I start looking around for help. Of course Gladys doesn't hear any of this. The only person I see is Mr. Unfriendly heading towards me with a young woman. He speaks quickly to her and she runs closer.

"Boku Weah wants to know what is going on. Is someone bothering you?"

"There's fucking ducks in here and they won't leave."

Weah stops mid-stride before putting his foot down a six feet from my rice bag shower. He speaks to the young lady in dialect and she responds in kind. She stumbles over the words fucking ducks. There must not be a translation or she doesn't know what it means and has to say it verbatim.

"Fooking ducks," she says again and looks back at me. "Right?"

Shit. I wonder if women cuss down here. "Close enough. Ducks! A whole family of ducks. And they won't get out and the mother duck is yelling at me."

I'm watching the little ducks and the mother duck and my neck feels like I'm at a tennis match. I have to be ready to kick one if it gets too close. Weah looks at me and I'm glad the rice bags are opaque. He speaks to the translator again.

"You are afraid of ducks, Boku said?" she tells me.

"I'm naked in case he hasn't figured that out. And they are drinking the water in here."

Another rapid spate of words and then, "Boku says, all of this noise for ducks? I don't believe this. Of course they're drinking the water, they need water." She looks down at her feet then back up at me and says, "He said that, not me"

"I know sweetheart. He's mean like that. Tell him they can have all they want when I'm out of here."

Mr. Macho says something then turns and walks away, leaving me with the ducks from hell. The translator is running in the opposite direction from Old Hateful. The little ducky ones are continuing to follow the path of the water. The mother is keeping her distance while continuing to watch over her ducklets. Occasionally she would glance my way and give me the evil eye.

Mother Ducky lets loose some squawking and gets her children's attention. They head towards me. I am left to defend my honor against a duck. I pick up a bucket and as she gets close enough to do damage to my extremities and maim me for life, I toss part of the contents on her.

Too late I realize I may have to beat some ducks to death with my half empty bucket if I want to escape unscathed. I am standing naked on my rock with the bucket over my head ready to bring it down on the first little ducky that gets close. A little scrawny kid about five or six years old in orange shorts, no shirt and barefoot slips under the plastic wall. Everyone and every duck stops.

"You're not white," he correctly states, as he looks me up and down.

The mother duck runs towards him and he scoops her into his arms. The babies also run in his direction and it doesn't take a genealogist to figure out they belong to him.

He stares at all of me, and tilts his head to one side.

"Are these your ducks? You should keep them out of decent people's bath. They could have hurt me."

"They're just ducks," he says with a disgusted look at me. He frowns his little face before he says again, "You're not white."

"I never said I was."

"Boku Weah said to get the ducks from the white woman in the bath. You're not white."

"Well that shows you Boku Weah doesn't even know his colors."

Now the immediate danger is over, my adrenaline level is returning to normal. Why am I having a conversation with a little boy while I'm naked and he is surrounded by ducks? This is a little awkward.

"Don't you think you should leave?"

He stares at me a little more and I bring my bucket down to cover the hairy part.

"I wanted to see the white woman, but there's only you and you talk funny."

"Well at least I'm not holding a duck and I think you talk funny too. How come you can speak English?" I point out with all of the maturity of a fifty-five year old woman naked in a shower talking to a six year old.

"These are my ducks and when they get big I'm going to sell them and save the money so I can go to school so when I get big I can be a doctor and help people. I need to speak English for when I go to college. Everybody knows that."

On that note, he turns, with his mother duck in his arms and six little ducklings following and leaves me to finish my bath. I have half the water I started out with and my P, T and A left to wash. I do the best I can with the water remaining to knock the funk off those areas. When my dress and shoes are on, I call long and loudly for Gladys.

"Oh my. Boku Weah was very upset. He talked strongly to me. Sorry, sorry for the ducks. Isaiah is getting in trouble right now for not keeping up with his ducks. His brother Brian is trying to take the blame, but it's not working. Isaiah was supposed to watch the ducks since they are his."

"But he's so little."

"Yes but he has to be responsible for his property. If he is not responsible, how can we expect him to go to school?"

"Gladys, why would Weah tell him I was white?"

"He didn't say you were white. He said you were quee. Well, it is the same thing."

"Could you share the reasoning with me? What does he mean, I'm quee?"

"Sorry, sorry. A quee woman is a white woman, or a woman who doesn't belong here. They are women from America or other places besides Africa. But you belong here," Gladys assures me.

"Thank you for saying so Gladys," I tell her while turning to leave.

How dare he. Who is he to say where I belong. I could belong here. If it weren't for the ducks. And the pigs. And the mosquitoes. And the heat. Maybe I don't belong in this particular village, but I could very easily adjust myself. If I wanted to live here.

I see him on the other side of the compound and head towards him, ready for battle. Even if he can't understand me, I'll feel better giving him a piece of my mind. My stride is delayed by an elderly woman shoving a chicken in my face. Being a city girl, I don't know how to react. The only live chickens I'd ever seen were the baby chicks at Easter time. The nice little yellow soft smooth pretty ones.

This chicken was not nice judging by the noises coming from his sharp beak. He didn't look very soft and his feathers were definitely ruffled. He may have had an aversion to being held upside down with his legs tied together with a thin rope. Or he could have been upset at the way the old lady was shoving him in my face while speaking way too much dialect for me to understand.

The duck owner appears and with all the arrogance of a child says, "She is giving you the chicken as a gift. She says thank you for coming."

Smart ass kid. I could tell from the look in his eyes he knows I am as afraid of chickens as I am of ducks. "Tell her I said thank you very much. It is a wonderful chicken."

I don't know what he told her but she continues to hold the chicken in my face and starts to shake it. "Did you tell her what I said?"

"Yes, she wants you to take the chicken," he says with a smirk. He stands back to watch me.

There is one thing that is not going to happen. I have never held a bad tempered upside down chicken in my life and I have no intention of starting now. I probably can't smack this kid upside the head either and since he is the only one around to communicate with her, I have to be nice to him.

"Look kid, we both know I'm scared of the damn chicken. So why don't you take it for me?"

He reaches out to take the chicken and says something else to the woman. Then he takes me by his other hand and walks me away. I smile at the chicken gift lady and walk with my new protector. "Hey, what am I supposed to do with the chicken?"

He looks up at me and smiles. "Kill it, we'll eat it."

I smile back and tell him, "Take it to the house and ask them to cook it and we will definitely eat it." The chicken lets out some rather loud upset noises as if he understood what we were planning for him.

"You are very nice. Would you really boil me like Boku Weah said?"

"Boil you! That's ridiculous. Of course I wouldn't boil you."

"Boku Weah says that is what quee women always do and I should tell others to stay away from you so we don't go missing."

"Thank you very much for telling me." I remember where I was going and disengage my hand. I look around and spot my prey again. "I'm going to go have a little walk. Please take our chicken to the kitchen."

He walks away swinging our chicken and I head towards Weah. "I wish you would learn how to mind your own business. I know you don't think I belong here, but I can be here if I want to, and there is nothing you can do about it."

He stares at me and says not one word.

"Oh I forgot, you don't speak English. If there was someone around, I'd have them tell you I hope your dick receives the bites from a thousand mosquitoes and there is nothing and no one to come to your aid and it itches and hurts so bad you would beg someone to cut it off. Then maybe you wouldn't be so damn mean."

He continues to give me the long blank stare followed by a slow blink of his eyes.

I remember the wonderful curse and end my tirade with, "You damn native man!" and turn to leave when a deep firm voice asks me.

"What did you just say?"

Who the hell is talking? I thought we were alone. When I turn back around, we are alone, which means only one person could have asked the question. "Did you just speak to me in English? Perfectly good English."

"Is that not the language you speak?" Weah is staring me straight in my face. He looks as angry as the mother duck recently removed from my shower.

"Why have you been pretending you can't speak English when you can?" I think back over all of the horrible and all of the revealing things I had said to him and my blood boils hotter.

"I never said I could not speak English. I chose to help others learn English by translating. And, I do not want to talk to you. I want you to leave."

"And I want you to kiss my ass. I am sick and tired of men thinking they can define me or tell me what to do, what to wear, or for that matter anything else. You just better watch it Buster, or I'll, I'll, I'll do something you don't like."

"Don't you ever call me a damn native man again, you, you damn Yankee."

"Who the hell calls somebody a Yankee? That doesn't even make sense. You're pretty stupid if Yankee is the best you can come up with." I lift my nose in the air for a sniff and to let him know what he was saying didn't mean shit to me.

Weah voice goes from bass to soprano and he starts to sweat. "Stupid. Stupid. You call me stupid? A man who got you from Monrovia to Middletown. You would call me stupid. I, who get up in the morning and dress myself, you would call me stupid." His arms are moving and he is now looking as pissed off as I am feeling.

"If the shoe fits wear it," I tell him on a parting shot.

This time when I'm finished I turn and stomp back to my room. I see Alita and immediately walk to her. "Why didn't you tell me Weah speaks English? He heard everything I've been saying to him."

"Of course Weah speaks English. He was educated in the States. Why did you think he didn't?" Alita looks puzzled.

"Alita, you never speak to him in English."

"Because we prefer to speak our dialect. I was not aware he never spoke to you. So sorry dear one, but where is the harm?"

"Oh Alita, you wouldn't believe the things I've said. This is terrible."

"I know you do not like him..."

"It doesn't matter. I've just said some embarrassing things to him thinking he didn't know what I was saying."

"Lynn, maybe you like him more than fine, no."

"What difference does it make? When I said he was stupid for calling me a Yankee, he was pretty damn angry."

"You called him stupid? Oh, Lynn." Her eyes get very round and her mouth opens. No words come out of her mouth.

"Stupid doesn't seem so bad," I tell her.

"Lynn, the second worst thing you can call a Liberian man is stupid. It means he is totally without sense, he is hopeless and of no use."

"Well I'm batting a thousand Alita, because I called him the worst thing too."

"Don't tell me you called him a damn native," Alita stops to say.

"Okay, I won't. But that's how I found out he could speak English."

Alita starts shaking her head. She makes a tsking sound and comes over to me. "Come; let's go back to the house. What happened?" She puts her arm around me and we start walking.

I explained my duck bath and ended with "Well I didn't intend to call him names. He's mean and I'm sick of his shit."

"I understand. Lynn, right now you may want to get dressed, for the false burial will start soon."

"Alita, do I have to apologize? I may have acted irrationally."

"Let it rest, I will speak with Weah. Go now to get dressed."

"Will you tell him I'm sorry? I was angry."

"I will also tell him he should not have allowed you to think he could not speak English."

Alita leaves and I go in to get dressed in my black outfit. When she comes in an hour later she says, "Everything is fine. Weah accepts your apology and sends his own apology in return."

"Thanks Alita, I appreciate your help. Is it time for the false burial? The bells are ringing."

"Yes, let us leave now."

We exit and the setup is almost the same as last night. The main difference is the men are sitting and the drums are smaller. Weah is sitting on the side of me Gladys occupied last night. He tries his best to sit far enough away that our bodies do not touch.

There is a woman who can only be described as very old in the middle of the open space. She has on a lappa suit, a piece of fabric in her hand, and a whistle is in her mouth. She gives a signal to the drummers and they start the beat. She blows shrilly on the whistle three times and the drummers pick up the beat. Women come from the different areas of the compound.

They are all dressed in the same fabric, a wrap skirt and top with a large neck that exposes one shoulder. They have a piece of matching fabric in their hand. Everyone has an anklet made with large shells that make noise on both ankles. The old woman with the whistle blows and points. The women follow her direction and dance with more energy than I had at twenty. They dip, rise and keep in constant motion. They come to dance in front of us. The older woman blows the whistle. Young girls in matching skirts rush forward with the ankle bracelets in their hands.

Weah deigns to explain. "The women are offering to allow you to dance with them. The yallowa is to wear on your ankle as a sign of unity and to announce to all you are a member of this village. If you choose to dance, you will raise your lappa slightly and the girls will put the yallowa on your ankle. If you chose not to dance, you wave them away. They will understand. There are not many quee women who are offered the opportunity, and fewer still that accept the challenge."

Alita has her lappa lifted slightly and is tapping her foot as the yallowa is being attached. I roll my eyes at Weah then lift my skirt and motion for one of the girls to come forward. As she bends and starts tying the heavy shells strung onto cord above my foot, I notice Weah looking at me.

"Quee woman, what do you think you are doing?"

"The least I can do is dance for him. Even a quee woman can dance."

I stand and follow Alita and Comfort to join in the women dancing. They come to hug me and give me a scrap of cloth. I imitate them and wave it in the air then bend low and move. The dancing continues and after ten minutes I'm ready to sit my tired ass down. We move in a line, and then into a circle, all the while the little old harridan keeps blowing the damn whistle. We have to keep moving.

The weight of the yallowa is making it difficult to lift my feet. The other women, Alita included show no signs of fatigue. Had I known how long they planned to dance, I would have waited longer to join in. A glance at Weah shows a smug smile on his face, as if he could see the pain in my feet. Him seeing me quit is not an option, so I lift my leaden arm to wave my fabric with the other women. Finally,

finally, the whistle stops and so does the drumming and it is time to sit down.

The other women run off except for Alita, Comfort and I. We return to our seats and I wipe the seat pouring like a waterfall from my head. The whistle blower and other older women return with three bowls of water and three straight razors.

"It is time for the cutting of the hair," Weah tells me before getting up and walking away. He goes to stand with a group of men under the almond tree.

Gladys has come to assume her position. She is sweating from the dance and her rapid breathing makes it difficult for her to speak. "Lovely dance, lovely dance."

An old stooped woman leaning on a stick taller than she is walks forward to stand before Alita. When she opens her mouth she speaks in the dialect.

"We are here for the false burial of our son. Will you have your hair cut to honor his memory?" Gladys interprets.

Three men step forward and Alita shakes her head before she speaks and pulls out money from her ample bosom. The money changes hands and the men go back to stand with the same circle of men Weah is standing among.

Alita speaks and Gladys tells me, "Alita says her husband is honored by the dance. Her hair was his joy and she will buy her hair to honor his memory."

The old woman moves to Comfort and repeats the question. A man from the circle steps up and at a nod from Comfort comes forward.

He says, "I will pay for the hair of this woman."

The old lady comes to me and Weah makes a step forward. I pull out my money and start talking before he can come any close. "This money is offered for the hair I would leave in memory of the one we came to bury. Thank you for your acceptance of me and allowing me to be a part of this event."

The money transfers hands. Weah frowns and returns to his circle. Alita looks over at me and smiles. Comfort hugs me. The women all celebrate and the bowls of water and razors are removed. We return to our seats.

The village chief comes forward. He speaks and according to Gladys, he wants to know if we will be leaving the family or selecting a husband. Alita stands and goes over to where the women are standing. She reaches down to remove a toddler from his mother's arms. "This will be my husband. He will stay with his mother until the time is right."

The mother of the child Alita is holding starts crying and thanking her. She kisses Alita on both cheeks, assured her son will be able to attend school and have a chance to succeed outside the village. Alita takes the child back to the chief.

The chief removes the baby and gives him back to his mother. Then he asks the mother, "Do you agree to raise him until the time is right?"

The mother vigorously shakes her head in the affirmative.

The chief moves to stand in front of Comfort. They have the same conversation and she walks over to the circle of men to select one. Not surprisingly, it is the same man who paid for her hair. She says to the gathering, "I choose this man."

The man says, "My cousin kept this woman for many years. She is a strong woman and I wish her to remain as my wife."

When he gives the chief money, the crowd cheers and claps. The chief takes both of their hands. He raises them and asks, "Will the family agree for this union to occur?"

The people cheer louder and louder.

The chief says, "Let the union be recorded." He clasps their hands together and lifts them over his head. He lowers their hands and steps back.

The man kisses Comfort before the chief takes one of each of their hand to join them. He lifts the joined hands above their heads and says, "Our village welcomes this union."

The chief comes over to me. Alita had explained I could select a husband or leave the village. Since this is my first and probably only visit, leaving won't be a problem. But I want a husband.

Once he has finished speaking I respond. "My next husband is here. I have selected him."

I walk over to the circle of men under the almond tree. Weah looks at me as I get closer. His eyes open wider and his mouth falls open when I slow down in front of him. When I pass him, his head snaps back as though I had struck him. I continue past him to the group of children standing close by. I select the one I believe would one day make his village proud. Even if it means raising ducks.

"Come to me," I tell him and hold out my hand.

He puts his duck down to run my way and place his hand in mine. We go back to the chief amid the laughter and cheers of people in the village. Except one person, Weah. He is looking daggers at me and I resist the urge to stick out my tongue.

A woman comes forward, crying and hugging me. The chief asks the same questions he had asked of Alita and we all agree he will stay with his mother until the time is right. Weah is still frowning.

Alita gives the chief the gifts we have brought for the village. The gathering is now ready to eat. The food is rice served under interesting shades of orange and green toppings.

"Gladys, tell me about the food," I ask my personal helper.

The orange is palm butter, our native food. The palm nut is put in a mortar and covered with hot water. It is beaten and then strained. The green are the leaves of the cassava, a root similar to a potato. The leaves are cut very fine and boiled. All have meat or fish and the palm butter has kissme."

"What is kissme?"

She stirs around in her dish and brings out what looks like a black rock. She puts it to her mouth and sucks something through the hole at the top. "You have to kiss it to eat it so my people call it kissme."

I find one and mimic her actions. A piece of something flies into my mouth, slightly salty and a little chewy. Not bad. My fork comes across something dark and finger sized. "What is this Gladys?"

"Meat," she tells me.

"Oh. What kind of meat?"

"Meat. Just meat."

It's probably better to operate on a need to know basis and I don't really need to know. It may be a good idea not to ask for any more specifics after Alita's cat comments. The food is all different and spicy but it is a grand adventure to be eating under the African sky. Thankfully the meal comes with a glass of thick water Gladys said comes from the young coconut.

Through the meal I can feel Weah watching me intently. Each time I look directly at him, he looks away. If he weren't such a mean person, we could be more than friends. The sun is setting by the time we finish.

Slowly the gathering breaks up as the shadows of night cover the sky. Alita, Gladys and I go to our temporary home and spend a short time talking. Alita and Gladys retire and I stay sitting on the hard couch. The night continues to intrude and brings a feeling of sadness. Tomorrow we go back to Monrovia. The next day we leave for Paris and then it is time for me to go home.

I don't want to remain indoors so I go out to the fire hot where Alita spoke to the ancestors. Alita told me the family relationship still exists, but I don't consider him a husband, and my navel string is not buried here. It is difficult to explain how he is a part of my life, even to myself. I take a seat on the ground to close a door on my past and have a final conversation with a special man.

"I just wanted to tell you thanks. You helped me to know myself. I'm sure you expected me to come and see you again, but I couldn't. It would have gone sour at some point and ruined the memories." I think about what else I would like for him to know if he were still here and continue to talk to him.

"Thank you for introducing me to an incredible woman. Alita was the perfect wife for you. She understood you. I could not have done the same. But know that you made a difference in my life and I will miss you." Tears are slowly rolling down my cheeks and I don't bother to wipe them away.

A movement just past the firelight catches my eye. "Who's there?"

Weah steps into the weak light from the flame to ask, "Why aren't you in bed?"

"I couldn't sleep. I'll be going in soon. Why are you still up?"

"I'm restless so I wanted to walk around the village."

The silence that follows is awkward. I want to talk to him, really apologize for my earlier behavior and try to understand why he is so hostile to me. "Can I walk with you?"

He holds out his hand, "Come to me."

I put my hand into his and allow him to assist me to my feet.

"Tell me about life in the village."

"What do you want to know?"

"Whatever comes to your mind."

We start walking and he explains the workings of Middletown to me, all the while with my hand nestled in his. "The chief lives on the other side of the rock. When there is a misunderstanding the chief goes out to the sea and listens to the waves to get wisdom. The high priest also lives there. Outsiders are not welcome in the home of the high priest."

"My people believe animal blood can still take away any wrong and cause crops to grow. When they are ready to go on the farm, they make a sacrifice to the rock so the rock will bless them to make rice.

When anything happens, they go to the rock, cook rice, kill a cow and on a certain place on the top of the rock they leave the food. When the birds come to eat what is offered, we say the rock has accepted the food. During difficult times, if the birds did not eat the food, they believe the sacrifice was not accepted.

"When they make the sacrifice and go out to harvest the food from the farm, the first rice cut from every farm is tied by bundle. It is taken to town and the high priest cooks it and presents it to the rock. Then the real harvest takes place. The Christians do not give the sacrifice of first fruits. The Christians believe that once you plant whatever you want to plant, in November there is a thanksgiving. They all bring the first fruit to the church. The reverend will bless the first fruits. It is split in half. One half is then sold. The other half is given in baskets to the destitute."

When he finishes talking, we are at the edge of the water. The waves are gently coming in and going out.

"Why did you come here? Alita told me you were only with him once. Did you love him that much?"

"I came because it seemed the right thing to do. Did I love him that much? How much is that much?"

Maybe it is because it is nighttime. Maybe it was because we are on the water's edge in Liberia in a remote village. Whatever it is, I start talking. "We connected. He was like a drug and if I had never had a part of him, my life would still be my life, but less full. I can't explain it any better than that."

We continue to hold hands and look out at the ocean. After a while, I have the courage to ask him about himself.

"What about your wife?"

"She chose to remain in Minnesota instead of returning to Liberia. She was enamored of the place. I hated it, the cold, and the need to attempt assimilation and bury my culture. But she embraced the newness of America. She acclimated herself very well until you could not tell her from a quee woman. She took a man into our home and slept with him in our bed. That was the end of our marriage. I have not spoken with her in years."

"She must have hurt you deeply."

He doesn't bother to reply. Instead he turns us to head back. He stops at the door to the house and looks at me. I look up at him and we slowly start to bend in towards each other. Alita opening the door causes us to jump apart. She looks at our hands still clasped and turns to go back into the house.

"Goodnight Lynn." He disengages our hands and leaves.

Alita is in the small sitting room, "Lynn, I didn't mean to interrupt. I saw you at the fire hot earlier and when I looked again, you were no longer there."

"It was nothing. Nothing at all."

"It looked like much more than nothing, Cherie."

"I'm finally sleepy now. See you in the morning."

The next morning we are up early to prepare for the drive back to catch our ship. My shower is duck free and I dress in a tie dye dress. Weah comes in to get our belongings and barely speaks. Alita sees and gives one of her African-Gallic shrugs. I try to remember I do not like him at all, but after last night, it is hard. Outside the villagers gather for our departure. There is another speech from the chief and the instruction for us to return.

My new husband Malachi has his mother duck in his arms, ensuring the little ones stay close. His long eyelashes are quickly filling with dampness from his tears. I smile at him and give him a small wave.

He turns to the older boy next to him and shoves mother duck into the boys' hands then runs towards me. "I have to tell you something." I bend down for his important proclamation. He takes a deep breath and tells me, "I will make you proud you chose me." He gives me a hug and then runs back to his ducks. He retrieves the mother duck from his friend and then waves before turning away to wipe his eyes.

THE BEGINNING OF THE END

In twenty minutes we are on the road. My eyes get heavy quickly. Soon they are closed. Gladys wakes me up when we reach the city. A few hours later, we are back on board the Rusty Bucket heading to Monrovia. Weah has studiously avoided me. I go to my room and he enters behind me.

"If you should feel sick, take some slow sips of water. I told the Captain about the roach that was here before. He assures me the cabin has been cleaned. I will check on you later." He gives me the bottle of water and leaves before I can utter a sound.

I stay in my room and when Alita comes in, she is ready to talk. "Lynn, what did I interrupt between you and Weah?"

"Nothing, we were just talking."

"Cherie, Weah is an angry complicated man, but he is just a man."

"What does that mean?"

"I mean, if he is the one you want, take him. He is angry because he does not want to feel the desire. That anger is directed at you. There is much passion between the two of you. Embrace it."

"Even if what you're saying is true, he hates me, or at the least doesn't like me and wants me to leave. Last night he held back and even if you hadn't come, I doubt he would have completed the kiss. He ran away when you came."

"If you risk nothing, you have nothing to gain. Maybe he does not see how much he wants you. It's up to you to show him."

Her words call me to be more active in the pursuit. He looks like he would be worth the chase and I enjoyed our conversation in Maryland. "Maybe I will Alita, maybe I will."

"Dare to try."

Alita and I walk around the ship and have a late afternoon meal with the captain and Weah. It is his first appearance since we boarded. The captain is doing his hand squeeze finger flex at my breasts until Weah looks sternly at him and says something in dialect. Whatever he said causes Alita to smother a laugh and the captain to fold his hands.

Alita tells me, "Now we are finished eating you may want to rest. The jolts of travel can make one exhausted."

"I'll close my eyes and might even fall asleep," I tell her before excusing myself to my host and Weah.

There is no living creature to disturb the slumber that doesn't come. Sleep evades me and after hours of looking out of the portal, we are in port. Weah gets us back to the house without sharing any conversation with me. He speaks some in dialect to Alita in order to deliberately exclude me from the conversation.

Alita turns to tell me, "Weah will make plans for our departure. He is a little shy and doesn't want to speak."

Weah's face goes into the familiar frown," Alita, you know-."

Whatever he wanted to say Alita knows is interrupted when Wilhelmina and Woapla run out of the house for hugs.

"Auntie Lynn, a man called looking for you. He said he met you at the airport and you were to have dinner together," Wilhelmina tells me.

My erstwhile suitor had been erased from my memory during my adventures in Maryland County. I look over at Weah. His habitual frown is back in place. He directs dialect to Alita.

She laughs and says, "Lynn made a conquest when we first arrived. He gave us his direction so he could get to know her better."

He says something else and Wilhelmina and Woapla both gasp. Alita's smile is non-existent and she turns to confront him.

"Weah, you are being ridiculous. Wilhelmina and Woapla, go into the house." After they are gone Alita continues, "Furthermore Weah, I will not allow you to insult my mate in such a fashion. You do us no honor with your words."

"Alita she is trouble. You should have never asked her to come here."

"In case it escaped your notice, she is a grown woman," Alita shoots back.

At those words I stand a little straighter and throw my shoulders back. "You know what Alita; maybe dinner wouldn't be such a bad idea. After all, I leave tomorrow. But I may even like this guy. I'll get his number from Wilhelmina. Would you like to come with me?"

Alita looks at Weah then back at me. "Dinner sounds intriguing."

Weah says nothing, instead moving the luggage inside. When it is settled to his liking, he speaks. "I hope you enjoy your dinner. As you say, you will be leaving tomorrow."

"Alita, I'll just go make the call." I brush past Weah and allow my breasts to graze his arm. He looks at me and I smile before continuing indoors.

When Alita comes in a short time later. "Cherie, are we going to dinner or were you merely inciting Weah."

"I don't want to go to dinner. I'd rather stay here. I just wanted to piss Weah off."

"You did a good job of achieving your goal. He is in a state of upset. Are you sure there was nothing I interrupted in Middletown?"

"If you hadn't come when you did, I'm pretty sure he would have kissed me."

"And what would you have done should the kiss had occurred."

"Alita, I would have let him. And kissed him back. He pisses me off, but damn, he is appealing"

"Then you are sorry I intruded?"

"It's probably a good thing you did interrupt. I don't need complications when I can maybe have my old life back." As soon as the words come out it occurs to me this has been my first thought of Robert since Paris.

Woapla comes out and says, "Old Ma, Auntie Lynn, dinner is on the table."

Alita keeps up lively chatter through dinner to remove the pall of our impending departure. One more day and then it's time to leave. Funny now that my time here it is almost over, the heat is bearable and the mosquitoes aren't interested in me anymore. After dinner we retire for the night. The bed is welcoming after the amount of travel my body endured.

In the morning the daylight wakes me. The African sun comes through every crack in the curtains at the window. A breeze is flowing through the room and my thoughts turn to the man who used to live here. My stomach growls to let me know it's time for breakfast. The musings are pushed to the side so I can search for sustenance.

In the dining room there is only Weah. I look at him and think how wonderful he would look naked. How his skin would feel, how the hair on his chest would look and how his nipples would feel in my mouth or vice versa. His beard would chafe my cheeks and when he sucked on my new breast with extra pointy nipples, the mustache would lightly cause friction. If he put his head between my thighs, the sensation would make me scream.

He turns his head and looks into my eyes. "Your eyes are a window into your soul. I can see what you want."

I decide to brazen out his statement. "I don't know what you mean. I was just looking at you."

"It's not just you looking at me, it's the deep look. You see way too much and what you want shows on your face."

"What do you think I want, Weah?"

"I think you want me."

"And why would you think something so absurd?"

"Because I see it in your eyes. I see the desire."

He is right. I want him with an intensity I had not felt in years. My breathing alters in response to the electricity running through the air. For the first time since Monaco, I want a man. This man.

The problem is I don't know exactly what I want from him. The opportunity to have casual sex is appealing, but so is something more. If I give in to the temptation or can convince him to lower his guard enough to allow this to happen, will it be enough or too much.

I'm afraid he would be like an apple you start eating and it's so good you want to keep eating. But it's too big and you don't know if you can finish it. And if you do finish it, how long will it be until you can get the next bite.

Alita had told me in Monaco to wait until it was worth it, wait until it was someone who would be memorable. Weah would be memorable. Thoughts of getting my life back get pushed to the back of my mind. One thing I remember is the anticipation with Mr. M.O.P. before we actually consummated our relationship.

The thought of making love with Weah makes my extra perkies tighten at the thought of his mouth covering them. The space between my legs gets damp at the thought of his magnificent hands with the thick, blunt fingers entering the heat radiating from the juncture. My eyes drift to those hands. I can see his arm holding me up and his hand stoking my back, low, just above ass level. His other hand is coming around and lifting my lappa. The only thing under the lappa is the strand of beads I had made at waterside. The three rows heat in expectation. He does not disappoint me in my fantasy.

His hand pulls and tugs the beads, rubbing them, tightening and loosening and creating a path of surrender wherever they come in contact with my skin. His hand slips lower and makes a trail of heat to the top of my thighs. His fingers remind me of the tentacles of an octopus, able to bend and maneuver around all of the curves and under the folds into the crevices. He parts me and slips a tentacle into the cavern that is waiting for his entrance.

A sound from deep in my front brings me back into the room. He looks at me as if he has read my thoughts and can see the visions I'm seeing of him with his hands underneath my lappa. I breathe in and smell the essence of my arousal in the air. The breath leaves and when it returns I smell the scent of his arousal. I step closer to him and his salt and pepper hair begs me to touch it. His scent is clean. Like sunshine. The lines at the corners of his eyes appear as he narrows his gaze. Looking into them, I see the heat. His nostrils flair and he picks up my scent.

"Stop," he yells and causes my eyes, I don't remember closing, to pop open.

"Stop what?"

"Stop looking like that and stop looking at me."

"Why?" I remember Alita's words.

"I don't like you. I want you to leave."

"Then ignore me," I tell him before picking up a piece of toast and leisurely putting jelly on it.

"I wish that I could."

"You can. The door is not locked. There is nothing keeping you here."

"I waited for you for a reason"

"What is the reason?"

"To give you a message. I am glad you will be leaving Liberia soon. The false burial is over. You can go back to France or to Kansas, I don't care. I'm glad you are leaving."

"You said that last night so why are we having this conversation if you don't care."

"I want what is best for you and my cousin," he says with his eyes glued to my breasts.

"Right, and if I believed that, I'd be the next queen of England. For some reason, I don't see you looking out for my best interest." I throw my shoulders back a bit more, take a deep breath and watch his eyes follow the twins. Then I think about Monaco and the Auditory room.

"I just wanted to tell you how I feel," he says dragging his eyes back to my face.

I look at the bulge in the front of his pants. "If the feelings you are having could show on your face, we would be private. There would be no one within hearing distance, no one to hear you scream as you come, sounding like you are in the midst of the most intense orgasm you have ever experienced. Intense enough to make you forget all of the ones before and beg to come back to the space between my thighs because that is where you will find home, satisfaction and contentment. The space between my thighs that will offer you all of the warmth, all of the all of the present and all of the future you would ever want. I think that is how you feel."

"You are insane. That is why you should leave." He is as stiff and still as a granite carved statue.

I think about my time in Monaco and the thought of conversation being an appetizer. "You know Weah, I wish I had time to wait." I tell him in a whisper.

"Wait for what?"

"Wait for us to get this anger fuck out of the way so we can move forward to wherever life would take us. Wait for you to man up and acknowledge the attraction is here and it is worth sampling, at least once. Wait for you to move past your fear of an African American woman."

"I am not afraid of you," he scoffs.

"Yes you are." I walk about an inch from his body and put my hand on his arm when he starts to back away. "You think about us and the thought is the prelude to reality, Weah."

His eyes drift to half mast as my hand comes up to cup his cheek.

"But not now. I want you when you can think about where we are and nothing else but how good the reality will be when we take that step. Yes, we need to get this anger fuck over. Maybe you'll come to Kansas."

"Absolutely not, quee woman!" He snaps back to attention with all of his defenses back in place.

I pluck a sausage link from the bowl on the table and put my lips around it before pushing it halfway into my mouth. I slowly draw it out. "Think about it. This could be you." I rub the sausage slowly over my top then bottom lip before delicately pushing it into my mouth again.

My exit from the room is to save me from what could be an embarrassing moment. There is a strong temptation to have sex with him on the dining room table.

I go to my room and sit for a few minutes. The climate heat and my sexual heat are burning me up. When I'm calm again, I start packing. Our flight leaves this afternoon for Paris. When everything is packed, I go back to the kitchen. Alita is eating and drinking her coffee. Woapla and Wilhelmina are sitting with red eyes. Weah is nowhere in sight.

"Young ladies, when school is out, you will vacation with me in Paris. You know it is not possible for me to stay here."

They get up and hug her then turn to me.

Woapla says, "We hold your feet Auntie Lynn."

"Why would you hold my feet?"

"We hold your feet so you will return," Wilhelmina says.

"Thank you ladies. You have made me welcome."

"Promise you'll come back," Woapla pleads.

"I can't promise that. My home is in Kansas."

Alita intercedes for me, "Do not worry Auntie Lynn. She must do what is right for her. Now, off to school for you both."

There is renewed hugging all around then they depart. Alita and I spend the time until our departure discussing our trip. All too soon, Joseph is at the door. For some reason, I am rather disappointed Weah did not come to take us, but I refuse to ask Alita about him. He is nowhere in my life. He is Africa.

Our flight to Casablanca and then Paris is uneventful. I sleep most of the way. Tuesday, we arrive in Paris. My first order of business is to send an e-mail to my mother.

Hi Mom,

I'm back in France and didn't see any wild animals, except one. But he was housebroken. The ceremony was wonderful. Tell everyone hello and I'll see you soon.

Life, Love, and Liberia,

Lynn

MY LIFE BACK

My day consists of last minute shopping to get gifts for the family. I spend my last night in Paris walking around the garden, looking at the flowers that make me smile. When I finally go in, Alita is in the sitting room.

"So Lynn, do you plan to get your old life back."

"Alita, I don't know. I think I should at least try. I need a little more time to think about it. I'm not comfortable with the thought right now, but we'll see. I probably will pick up where I left off and try to make it work."

"Then I wish you well, Cherie."

Louis comes to the door. "Is there anything at all I can do for you," he asks the room with his eyes on me.

The only thing I can think of would have me needing another shower before I go to the airport. If I should ever return, it would be interesting to see just what "anything" entails.

"Nothing for me, Louis, thank you."

Alita looks at him and smiles. "Maybe later."

He gives a half bow and leaves.

All too soon, it's time to go to the airport. Etienne gets my luggage checked while Alita clucks over me. I doubt we'll ever see each other again and we hug tightly as if we both know it. I turn to go through security and my flight home.

After forever, the plane touches down. I'm back where I started, Wichita, Kansas. I am prepared to go forth and have my old life back. No more rusty bucket sailing, no chicken gifts, no pigs in bushes or ducks in my bath. The airport is tame in comparison to the other places this adventure had me going. There are no long lines anywhere and everywhere, everyone speaks English. I go to the familiar baggage claim area to get my suitcases full of memories before heading to ground transportation. The cab ride home is uneventful except everything seems flat, dull, without excitement or color.

As the cab pulls into the driveway, there are unexpected lights in the front room and on the second floor in my bedroom. Robert's car is in the driveway and mine is parked on the street. The only people that had a key are my parents and my middle daughter. How could he have gotten in and why the hell is he in my house? No one knew for certain when I was coming back, so how long has this bastard been laid up in my divorce settlement.

My key is in the door and the door hits the wall with such a force the house shakes. "Robert, what the hell is going on? Why are you in my house?"

He comes running from the front room. "Lynn, your language, it's so unbecoming. I thought you had gotten over that. You're home. I wasn't sure when to expect you No one did."

"How does when I get home explain why you're here?"

"You haven't written or called for over a week. And how did you get here from the airport? You didn't call me to come and get you."

"What are you doing here, Robert?"

"Well we talked about getting back together. Remember? I went ahead and came home so you won't be alone anymore." He walks closer to me, arms outstretched.

"Yes we talked about it, but no decision was made." I remain standing just past the doorway.

"I know how you hate being alone. Lynn, don't worry about a thing, I'm back now. May let me use her key when I explained we are back together."

"Robert, we really need to talk. There is a difference between now and when you first left."

"We can talk in the morning. Today is Wednesday."

"And?"

"You know what we do on Wednesday night, right?" He gives me a wink.

"Oh hell, my stroke night." Our nights for carnal activity are Sunday and Wednesday. It doesn't matter I'm just getting in from a transcontinental flight. Nothing can stand in the way of his routine. How could I have forgotten?

"What? I know it's been a while, but you won't have a stroke. That's funny."

"Yeah, funny, Robert. So is it over with you and Brenda?"

"She's not you, Lynn. She isn't you."

"Obviously she's not me. You left me for her."

"We'll talk later. Now come to bed. Just leave the suitcase down here. You can get them in the morning."

"I'm not the least bit tired. You go ahead up and I'll be there later."

Robert looks at me for two minutes, watching me as I walk around him and into the living room, noticing how the pictures I had hung on the wall have been removed and the furniture returned to the position it was in when we first moved into the house. He doesn't say a word, just watches me. My life back.

I give up trying to do anything and tell him, "Okay Robert. Let's go to bed."

He leads the way up the stairs after moving my suitcase into the corner. "What's in here? This seems heavy. Never mind, we can sort through the stuff tomorrow."

I hit the shower and join him in bed. It isn't quite nine o'clock. "What's been going on since I've been gone? How come you moved back here before we talked?"

"Nothing has been going on. I moved back because I didn't want you to come home to an empty house. Not that I've moved everything from the apartment just yet. We can get the rest of the things over the weekend."

"We? What the hell do you mean we? Am I supposed to help you move your things after you left me?" I sit up in bed to look him in the eyes.

"Lynn, really, this cursing is getting out of hand. We'll talk about your getting my things, I mean us getting my things later. Come on and lie down."

With those words of love, he climbs up to his missionary perch. He doesn't mention or maybe he doesn't notice my enhanced breasts. He gives me the full extent of his amorous ability and thirty-seven strokes. I may have miscounted because I dozed off in the middle of our activity and didn't wake up till he got out of bed to wash. Sleeps comes shortly after an overwhelming desire for a doughnut.

"Lynn, wake up. "You're on my side of the bed."

I wake up long enough to return to the farthest edge of my side of my bed. My life back, I think before going back to sleep.

Thursday my first telephone call after I call all the family, is to what may be my newest job, the next step on the stairway to our old life.

I dial the number and Jonathan answers on the second ring. "Hello Jonathan. This is Lynn Westner. Harold suggested you may be looking for a new assistant."

"Lynn, I've been waiting for your call. Can you come in tomorrow? We can talk salary and you'll be able to talk with Mykia to get an understanding of our system."

"Sure, how does nine a.m. sound?"

"Perfect. Mykia will be waiting for you and so will I."

Robert comes into the room as I hang up the telephone. "Who was that?"

"It was Jonathan, my new boss. I start tomorrow."

"Where? I didn't know anything about this. I'll do some research on the company and see if it's a place you should be working. What's the name of this place?"

"Robert, it's not your decision. I've decided I will work and I will work with Uster and McKinnon. If I don't like it I'll do something different."

"I already have a job lined up for you. You have to call Tolbert's. Here's the number, and ask for Damon. I told him you would call when you returned. Everything is set; I even got you a raise."

The voices in my head are clamoring for me to slap the man who broke my heart, or at least broke my life. He is coming back and picking up where he left off. He has probably convinced himself the whole divorce never happened. I take a deep breath and let it out.

"Robert please try to understand. As much as you think you know what is best for me, you don't. This is my decision and my decision alone. You must think you're coming home to the same woman you left. You're not. When and where I work is going to be my decision."

"Lynn I was trying to help. You know..."

"You were trying to control and it's not going to happen this time around." I think of my dream in Paris and the question Maya Angelou asked me. Am I really ready to come back to my cage? I don't know. I tell Robert, "And by the way, I'm still not convinced us getting back together is the best idea in the world."

I get my suitcase from its corner. It is a struggle to get it to the stairs. During this time Robert struggles to get the newspaper open. He sits on the couch and rattles the pages while I go bump bump with the suitcase on the stairs.

"No, Robert. I don't need any help taking this upstairs. You just keep on reading." He doesn't bother to look up from his paper. I could tell him to not bother wasting his time. It's fucking Wichita, there's nothing interesting or newsworthy going on.

I take my things upstairs and the scent in the clothing I start to unpack brings memories of what now seems like a different lifetime. I look at the lappa suit that almost got me attacked by a pig and the beautiful black suit made for the false burial. It occurs to me maybe Robert and I can't get back together since I have a new husband. Of course he is still in elementary school and he raises ducks. I look at the key to the suite in Monrovia. I have a place I can go to in another country if I want to go there. I put it the top drawer of my dresser.

The memories are becoming too much so I decide to go to my favorite restaurant to get a bite to eat. I head to the fast food spot place my order then get a seat to hear my group of old men and their conversation. Our first meeting or rather my first observation of them was during my divorce, right after Robert got stabbed. I was wasting time before going to my parents to explain how Robert got a hole in him and it really wasn't my fault.

The men were determining all the various uses of duct tape and solving the problems of the world. One member of their group was out so they also talked about him. Their missing member has returned. He is a gruff sort who is not hesitant to disagree with everything and everybody. A little listening brings me up to date on what they have been doing.

The current argument is over the oil spill in the Gulf. Each one of these guys has something different to say about this one subject. One even brings back the super strong all purpose duct tape as a way to solve the problem. They have more points of view than there are strands of hair on my head. If I had some friends, this could be me in ten to fifteen years; sitting in a fast food restaurant discussing the merits of traffic cameras, the futility of solar energy and the healing properties of cinnamon. My life back.

The vision is not as welcoming as it once may have been. I don't want to spend the rest of my life sitting in Wichita, Kansas and waiting for God's time as these men call death. I want to do something different. But what? Where could I go? I could join a travel club. I like traveling. Or I could try to do what I've wanted to do for years.

I could try to capture my dream and become a writer. I remember the home in Liberia, close to the water with a view of peace. I could go there and write until my heart is content. The money I got from my divorce settlement and the very lucrative severance package could keep me going for the next few years. I don't have to work at all.

With these thoughts on my mind I purchase a fried dessert and head back home. When I come in Robert is on the telephone. He hangs up as soon as he hears me and I have a sneaking feeling I know who was on the other end.

"Lynn, where have you been? I didn't hear you leave." He walks towards me.

"I went to get a bite to eat. Do you want some of my fried pie?" I go past him into the living room where I had been forbidden to eat when we were married and take a seat on the sofa. I put the bag on the coffee table and reach in to remove hot, greasy apple goodness.

Robert stands in the doorway. "You know we don't eat that stuff. Aren't you going to get dinner ready?"

"No, I'm not. I ate at the restaurant, which is why I am eating pie now. Do you want some? That's the last time I'm going to ask."

"Well what am I supposed to eat? Today is Thursday, and we usually…"

I cut him off to tell him, "You can eat whatever you like."

Having said my piece, I sit back on the sofa and turn on the television, open my fried pie and start munching. The nagging sensation regarding the telephone call causes me to pick up the handset and push redial. Sure enough Brenda answers on the first ring.

"Robert, come on back home. I said I was sorry."

"No Brenda, this isn't Robert. This is his wife. I mean ex-wife. He was using my telephone to call you. I'll give him your message though."

"Lynn, you're back? Robert said he was staying in your house alone."

"Robert lied. Go figure." I look over at Robert, still standing with the blood draining from his face. My face has a genuine smile before my hand replaces the phone in the cradle. "Old dogs and new tricks," I tell him.

"Lynn I can explain."

"No need Robert. If you explain, you would expect me to explain what I did on my trip. And that is not going to happen."

"What is that supposed to mean. I know you would never be unfaithful."

"We're divorced Robert. Me sleeping with someone would not be unfaithful."

"Forget about all of that Lynn, I trust you. Now come on. It's time to go to bed."

"You go ahead." I continue to watch television until I feel like going to bed. Robert had tried to get me to retire a few more times, but I refused.

The time to get up and go to work arrives earlier than anticipated. It's easy to pick out a standard blue suit with a common white blouse. At the last minute, I change the white blouse for a hot pink top that had been hanging new in the closet for a few months. The tightness across my new breasts puts pep in my step. It's hard to believe Robert had his nightly strokes and never even noticed the enhanced size. Well it's not so hard to believe. His focus is only on getting his. He is in the living room and stops me before the door beckoning my freedom gets open.

"Lynn, that top. The color is rather loud isn't it? I mean you don't want to wear something like that to work do you?"

"No, it isn't too loud and yes, I am going to wear it to my new job."

"Then it must be too small. Are you putting on weight? It looks a little tight across the top. Women tend to gain a little during times of stress and maybe you've been stressed. A lot of women become stressed when they go through a divorce. They let themselves go. It may be happening to you since our separation. I'll work on a menu to help you lose those pounds."

My hand is outstretched almost touching the doorknob. The same position it has been in since the comment about the color of the top. My back straightens as the steam coming from my ears almost sets off a smoke alarm.

"Robert, my choice of clothing is my own. When I start selecting your clothes, you may have more input on how I package my assets. And we didn't have a separation. We had a divorce. By the way, don't call your bitch on my telephone anymore. It's completely disrespectful." My hand goes completely around the doorknob and I exit while Robert is still talking.

I drive to my new job and park in their parking garage. There is a revolving door to get me into the building and the security desk where I have to pile my purse and lunch to be x–rayed. I ask the officer for directions to my new job, and armed with the information, head to the third floor.

Mykia meets me as I enter the office. "Lynn, it's so good to see you." She kisses the air around me and after looking me up and down, takes me in to talk with Jonathan. We settle on a salary that makes me blink. It is almost twice what I was making with Harold.

When I leave Jonathan's office, Mykia is there to show me around the office. There are rows of partitioned cubicles. After the fifth, it strikes me how similar each is to the other. They are all gray with one picture and the telephone on the desk. There are no decorations on the walls, nothing to break the monotony. Each person is wearing a black suit with a white top, men and women. If there is a difference, it is the men have on ties, but they are all black. If I look at the shoes, I'll bet they are all black.

I follow Mykia to our office. The only way to describe it is sterile. There is nothing personable about it and I imagine when she leaves,

I would be expected to move in and not change anything except the picture on the desk. In fact it is a replica of my old office. My life back.

She pulls out the organization chart and shows me where everyone fits. At ten thirty, her telephone goes off.

"Just my alarm, it lets me know it is time to go on break. I'll show you where the restroom is located."

I follow her from the office to the restroom. There is a line of people and we wait our turn. After the bathroom break we go to the vending area where we wait in another line for Mykia to get a nutrition bar then head back to the office. Two minutes after entering the door, her alarm goes off again.

"Just a signal the break is over," she says with a smile.

She settles in to showing me the contents of cabinets, locations of supplies, and updates on clients. Her telephone alarms again.

"Lunch time." We have to use our computer to sign out. She pulls up the timesheet program and waits.

"What are you waiting for?"

"We have to remain within a two minute window or it will cause an occurrence." Finally the time changes and she signs out. She gets her purse and I get mine. "We'll go around the corner since we have an hour."

At the restaurant, the hostess takes us to a seat.

"Ma'am, what will you have?" She has her pen at the ready as she waits for my decision.

"How about a bowl of lobster bisque?"

"You must be new at the firm," she says and smiles at me before she turns to my lunch partner. "Is it the Friday usual for you Mykia?"

"Yes thank you."

In minutes, the waitress is back with our lunch. "I know you need to get back on time, Mykia."

Our conversation is banal at best. Mykia talks about the job and what is to be done with each hour of her day. When we finish, we go back to work. The line to get into the building and through x-ray is long and I have the opportunity to look around the lobby. It is the same as the offices. Sterile.

Back at the desk, Mykia continues to point out duties within my purview. Open the mail in the morning, return calls in the late morning, and update files in the afternoon. In late afternoon, the alarm goes off again for a bathroom and vending machine break.

"Does everyone go to the bathroom at the same time?"

"We want everyone to be productive, so break time is bathroom time," Mykia shares.

At the end of the day, I feel like I'm emerging from a cocoon. As I'm trying to get out, the revolving door is full. The line behind me is patiently waiting their turn. It looks like a line of robots.

I head home. Robert's car is in the driveway and he is on the telephone. Smart money would say he is talking to Brenda. I go into the kitchen and the first thing I see is a menu on the refrigerator. He comes in behind me.

"I fixed the menus for the next couple of weeks. You look like you've put on a few pounds. This menu is low carb and will help with that little problem."

"I don't feel like cooking tonight, Robert. I may just go out to dinner."

"Then what will I eat?"

"You've been here all day and you didn't cook dinner. I guess you're not really hungry."

"Lynn, it's your job to cook dinner."

"If you think I'm cooking, one of the two people in this room is crazy as hell and it ain't me. If you're that hungry, you should have cooked. As a matter of fact, you should cook for you and for me since I'm the one going out to work every day."

"What?"

I go to the freezer and take out a toaster pastry. "Hey, you want one?"

"Those are full of sugar, they have no nutritional value."

"And that's probably why they taste so good." When it is in the toaster, Robert leaves the kitchen.

My pastry tastes great. I hear Robert leaving and feel nothing as much as relieved. I do get my coat on and go pull my car into the driveway. He doesn't have a key to my car anymore, so it will stay here until I move it in the morning.

Saturday, Robert wakes me up. "It's getting late. Don't you think we should get an early start getting my things moved here?"

"Here's a new rule Robert. If I'm sleeping, don't wake me up unless the house is on fire."

"Don't you want to help me?"

"No and I think moving anything else back here is premature. Let's wait till next weekend." I turn to my other side and refuse to budge.

Robert very noisily goes around the room slamming things and being childish. I stay in bed for the next two hours.

When I get up Robert is gone. I go to my parents. My father is out so my mother and I sit and talk about the activities during my absence and what the plans are now that I'm back home.

"Are you and Robert back together now?"

"I'm not sure Mom. It doesn't feel right."

"If it doesn't feel right now, what will make it feel right?"

"I don't know."

"Well baby, just don't let him be the elevator that brings you down. you've worked hard to get your life back on solid footing since that rascal did his dirt and left."

I think about climbing the Eiffel Tower and how my life has been since my return. He is bringing me down. Our sex life is lousy, our conversations non-existent. After kissing mom goodbye, it's back to my favorite restaurant to see what my old guys are talking about today. I get a burger and sit beside their table.

"Man I'm telling you, you can't use gum to hold a picture on the wall. It'll get hard and the picture has to fall."

"Not if you use bubble gum. Not that chewing gum stuff. That chewing gum isn't thick enough. Bubble gum, bubble gum will work."

"No it won't. I wish Lonell was here, he'd tell you a thing or two about gum."

"Yeah, I sure am gonna miss him. When's the funeral?"

"His wife said it'd be next Saturday. Can you imagine him having a heart attack?"

"Who would have thought he'd go so soon. He was only eighty-nine."

"Yeah, and he never did make it to Hawaii like he wanted to do."

"Man, that cat's been going to Hawaii for the past forty years and he never went."

"Now he never will."

They all sit silent with me watching them and looking back over my life decisions. It isn't long before the uneaten portion of my burger is tossed into the trash and I pull out of the restaurant parking lot and into my driveway.

There is a large flat package sitting unopened in the hallway when I enter the house. It is addressed to me and when I open it there is a note from Alita and an oil painting of the dinner we had with Brian, Patience and the fellows in her home.

I go in and put the furniture back they way I had changed it after the divorce. I don't see Robert so he's probably still pouting or back with Brenda. The funny thing is I don't give a damn one way or the other.

LOOSE ENDS

Sunday morning, I go to visit May. When she opens the door, I ask her, "Why did you give my house key to your father?"

"He said he needed to fix something for you. Then he told me you were getting back together. I'm so happy for you, Mom, come on in."

"May, we are not getting back together. He tricked you."

"But he said it was all settled. Let me get you a cup of tea. "

When she comes back she hands me a cup of something hot and red. May likes tea better than coffee and thinks it soothing. "I tried to ask you about it when you called, but we had a bad connection. So does that mean you're not getting back together?"

"May, your father lied. Nothing was settled and he should not have brought you into the middle of our discussions."

"I'm sorry. I was just so happy for you. I thought it was wonderful."

"Honey, I know you want what is best for me. It's time to let me make the decision. I feel a bit betrayed by you."

"Mom, I'm sorry. It's just things are changing so fast. It makes me scared. You and Daddy get a divorce, you don't have your same job, and you're traveling all over. I want things back the way they were."

"It can't go back to what it was, May. I've grown, your Dad's grown. Things are different. I still love you and I know your father does too. But we have to work this out according to what we feel is best for us."

"Okay, Mom. I love you too."

We hug tightly before I leave and visit the other girls and my parents. When I get home Robert has his car parked on the street for me to pull into the driveway. That is possibly his only concession to the new me because he starts in as soon as my key in the lock opens the door.

"Do you plan on following the menus, Lynn? I was expecting dinner to be ready."

"Not now or in the future, Robert. That was the old me."

"Well it's a good thing I ate at before I came home."

If I really cared, I guess I would ask him where he ate. I don't give a damn. I head towards the stairs.

"Don't forget its Sunday." When I look over at him, he has the nerve to wink at me.

'How could I forget Robert. You make it so good for me." When we have our sexual experience, I think about Louis. It makes the time go faster.

Monday morning comes and I head out to work early wearing a gray suit with a green shirt. I stop to get a doughnut before going into the office. Unfortunately when I get to work I find the color of the day at the office is a navy blue suit with a light blue shirt for everyone and blue ties for the men. Do these people call each other and say what they're wearing to work or what.

Jonathan calls Mykia and me into his office for some dictation and it breaks the monotony of the day. It's only been two days and I wish someone would do or say something, anything, exciting. The people are carbon copies of cardboard cutouts. By the second break of the day, I want to smash Mykia's telephone.

At home, Robert's car is in the driveway. He must be struggling to get used to the new parking routine. He greets me at the door. "Lynn, you're just getting used to a new job. You can wait and start cooking next week when you are more used to your routine."

"Thank you Robert. That's so kind of you. However, as I told you before, I do not plan to follow another menu now or in the future. If I feel like cooking I will, and when I do, I will cook what it is I want to eat. So what's for dinner?"

"I don't know. You can go pick something up."

"Why don't I order it and you can go pick it up. How does Italian sound."

"You're not going to go get it, Lynn?"

"No. but I will order some eggplant parmesan."

"Well, since you did just get home, I'll go get it this time, but you know how I hate restaurant food."

When he leaves, I move my car into my driveway. The fact does not go without notice.

"Lynn, your car is in the driveway and I can't move it because I no longer have a key," Robert says as he returns with our dinner.

"My car should be in the driveway. This is my house."

We have dinner and he stays stunned enough to be quiet. His mood changes to pouting and is evidenced by his refusal to answer when I offer him ice cream. I get some for me and then head to watch television. He goes to bed and plays sleep when I get in the bed on my side.

The next morning I think back over my previous job. I'm willing to bet the color of the day will be brown and get the brown suit with the cream shirt and the standard brown pumps out of my closet. Yes indeed, my old life back. I put on a green dress with green shoes with wedge heels and head off to work.

When I get there, the usual line to get in the door and past security is in place. Everyone has on a brown suit. Each suit wearer has a cream colored top. At their feet, they all wear brown shoes. The elevator takes forever and I make it to the office with one minute to spare. Punching a time clock, or in this case signing in on a computer, is stressful.

Mykia comes in a few minutes later and says, "I thought you would be here earlier. You're almost late and we always like for everyone to sign in at least five minutes before the start of their shift. It sets a good example."

At break/bathroom time I relieve my bladder and watch Mykia get the same damn bag of peanuts from the vending machine she gets every single time. At lunch, we go back to the same spot and she has the same lunch. The afternoon is a repeat of the other afternoons. I think I hate this place.

It feels as if I've been pardoned from the penitentiary when the day is over. The drive home is uneventful. Once again Robert's car is in the driveway. My life back is starting to feel overrated. Once in the house old habits have my feet heading to the kitchen.

It takes a few seconds for the menu on the refrigerator to register in my brain. When it does, I walk over and rip it to shreds without reading a word. Then my feet go in search of the bastard that put it there.

"Robert! We need to talk."

He comes down from upstairs. "Lynn, you're yelling. What is it? I was resting."

"Resting. You've had all day to rest."

"I had some errands to run, so I'm resting."

"Would your errand go by the name of Brenda?"

"Don't be silly." He immediately looks up, to the left, to the right, anywhere but directly at me.

"You know what Robert, this isn't working for me. The first time you cheated on me it caught me off guard. I can't see myself signing on for another go-round with my eyes wide open."

"Lynn, I know what you're thinking." He starts heading closer to me with his arms outstretched.

"Probably not." I back away from him.

"I understand you, I know you better than anyone."

"Unfortunately you don't understand ME like I do now. I doubt if you will ever be able to do what I need you to do."

"What do you need me to do?"

"I need for you to see me. To know that there is a complete woman here."

"I see you, Lynn."

"No you really don't. I could be a plastic doll for all of the attention you pay to the parts of me. When was the last time we kissed? Really kissed until we wanted to hold each other closer, tighter, longer"

"We kissed every day. When you went to work, we kissed. When we were in bed at night, we kissed. Now we're getting back together, we'll kiss more. Come here, I'll kiss you now."

"Robert, you don't get it. When was the last time we touched each other, really explored each other's body? When was the last time we did the things that turned each other on?"

"Lynn, don't be silly. We're old now. That's not important." Robert runs a hand through his thick head of hair and looks as lost as a watermelon at a grape convention.

"It's important to me. And it must have been important to you. What was it that attracted you to Brenda in the first place?"

"It doesn't matter, she's not you; and I want you back now."

"You didn't want me. Remember?"

"Lynn, you're being deliberately obtuse. Pay attention. The kids want us back together."

"The kids are grown. It really is about what I want, isn't it Robert. Right now, I'm not sure what comes next."

"I hope you don't have some ridiculous need to get revenge on me for Brenda. Besides, it's not like you have any other options. I'm your only choice."

"Hey, asshole, wake up. This is not about you. It's about me being sure of what I want to do for me."

"Lynn, you are being incredibly selfish. This isn't just about you. You have children."

"You had children when you left. As a matter of fact, you would have been perfectly content to see me go to jail for stabbing you just to get the damn divorce finalized so you could be with Brenda. Robert, you brought her into our home."

"Let's let bygones be bygones. We can make this work."

At one time I would have given his pronouncement the welcoming he believes it deserves. But not now.

"Lynn." Robert takes my upper arm and holds it lightly.

"Do not ever touch me again unless I ask you to touch me."

"You are my wife."

"I was your wife. I'm my own woman now and I am tired of this conversation."

"Lynn, listen to me." He does take his hand off my arm.

"No more conversation at all Robert." I walk to the door and open it for him to go through. Thankfully, he doesn't say another word.

The next day I call Jonathan. "Jonathan, thank you so much for the opportunity your position offers, however, I think it is time for me to retire."

"But Lynn, you fit so perfectly into our little family. Mykia can't say enough about how well you fit in."

"I certainly appreciate the offer and the compliment. I think I will take the time and do some traveling, enjoy my retirement."

"Well if you ever change your mind, give me a call."

"Thanks Jonathan."

My next call is to make plans for the termination of utilities and call Dottie. She gives me a reference for a property management company. I call and make an appointment with William from C.T. Duff Enterprises to discuss management of the property for the next year. William comes over the next afternoon. A nice looking brother, he is all about business.

After he looks around he asks, "Do you want to rent your property or sell it?"

"Well, I thought about renting it, but I don't know when I will be back."

"In renting, most people would want a lease of at least one year. Realistically, could you commit to being gone one year?"

"I don't know if I will ever come back here to live. I think if I do return to Wichita, I would want a smaller home, something that would suit me and only me. Maybe a home with one floor or a condo so someone else would have to worry about cutting grass or shoveling snow. There's no point in me keeping this huge house when everyone is gone except maybe me."

"You may want to consider selling the home and keeping the proceeds from the sale until you make up your mind."

"Then where would I go if I wanted to come home?"

"You can decide that when you return, or rent it and simultaneously put it on the market. Then if it sells, you have the money, if not; you may want to get a furnished condo for rent. You would keep your furniture in the condo and store those items you would not want used. Many businesses have condos they rent on a monthly basis for employees that will be here short term."

"Sounds interesting."

"We could make a lease work with one of those corporations. They would be responsible for any damages and with thirty days notice, you could terminate the agreement. The property would not experience the wear and tear of a straight rental, because it would only be used sporadically. A property in the downtown area would be ideal."

He tells me about more options and I make a decision. "Go ahead and arrange some showings."

William leaves and I call my parents to let them know I am on my way.

Once there, mom is in the kitchen cooking and dad is watching television.

"I need to talk with both of you."

When they are all in the kitchen, I break the news to them.

"I plan on moving to Liberia for at least a year."

My mother smiles and comes around the table to hug me. "Wonderful. It does my heart good for you to stand on your own and travel. Did you meet someone there?"

"I want to go and live on my own, get some focus."

My father is still sitting and staring at me like my new boob fell out on the table.

"What will you do there? Something could happen to you. What about your children?"

"Daddy, something could happen to me here. The children are grown, and I don't know what I'll do there."

"Baby, stop. You have to let her go. She's almost old as dirt. You can't protect her from everything and she will be all right. Do you need some money?" I love my mother.

"No mom. I decided to rent or possibly sell the house and was hoping you two would help me find a condo downtown. Then there'll be a place for me to go if I come back to live."

Dad stands up, "Where will you live when you come back?"

"Daddy, I'll always have a place to live if I buy a condo or a smaller house that suits me and is mine, without Robert memories."

"Lynn, you will always have a place to live. You can always stay with us, but don't sell your house. It's security."

"Thanks Dad. I don't think I'll need to move in here but it's nice to know I could." It's even nicer to know I don't have to come running home.

"You can always come home Lynn. Your mother is worried too."

"Baby, she has thought this through. You taught her that much. She isn't just jumping up and doing something without thinking. Lynn has given this a great deal of thought."

"How do you know? We have to look out for her best interest."

"I know because she is our daughter."

My mother walks over and hugs my father. He is struggling not to show any emotion but I see how tightly he is holding on to mom. I go over to him and hug them both.

"Dad I think I'll miss you the most."

My mother and I share a smile and understanding from under the bottom of his chin. He stands back, once again in command of himself.

"What else do you need us to do?" The sorrow and resignation in Dad's voice almost makes me want to change my mind.

"I haven't told the girls yet. How about a meeting at my house since it will be the last one for a while?"

"When?" Mom asks.

"Three days from now."

"We'll be there," Dad says.

"Have you told Robert?" Mom has a smile on her face.

"Robert had told me he wanted us to get back together before I went the first time."

"What did you say?" my dad asks.

"I told him we could talk about it when I got back. But here's what he did. He was at the house when I got back. He had told May we were getting back together and she gave him the key. I tried to see if it could work, but it was horrible. It was if he had never left and I realized I don't like him much anymore. He's gone again. I just told you two I'm moving to Liberia at least for a while."

Daddy says, "Honey you know we're here if you need us."

"Yes Dad. And I'm blessed to have the two of you for parents."

As I gather up purse and keys, I hear my dad whisper to my mom, "You don't think she's on some of those drugs like that girl of hers' said do you?

"No baby, she's fine. She's just growing up now."

"Oh. Well, you probably know better than I do. But what about Robert?"

"Good-bye to bad rubbish is my opinion. I never liked his pretty ass anyway." My mother turns her nose in the air and sniffs as only she, the queen of sniffs can do.

"It's time to head out and start planning the meeting with the children. I love you both. Bye now."

When the whole family finally does get together, I start the conversation.

"Ladies, I wanted to tell you all that your father and I will not be reuniting. Instead, I will be moving to Liberia."

"Moving where?" from Rene.

"Are you sure?" from May.

"Why?" from Lynette.

"Liberia, yes I'm sure, because I want to, at least for now."

"Mom, you just came back from there." Rene states.

"And I'm just going again."

EMBRACING PASSION

When the plane touches down I make it to the ground and into Roberts International Airport without help. When the immigration officer tells me how hot is, I agree and discreetly push a ten dollar bill his way. Without hesitation he stamps my passport welcomes me to Liberia. Ten dollars more in response to the weather comment gets my bags through customs unchecked.

Outside of the terminal, there are a plethora of cabs waiting. I enter the first and tell the cabbie, "I want to leave now, no more passengers."

"Where are we going?" he asks.

"Maude Barkley Estates."

"It will cost you twenty dollars U.S. if you charter the cab and I don't get any more passengers."

"Take me without stopping."

Our progress through Monrovia streets is slow until we get to the straight highway. Very little traffic is visible, being on the outskirts of the city.

"Auntie, are you coming to visit?"

"No I live here now."

"Is your husband Liberian?"

I think about Mr. M.O.P. and Robert, two completely different individuals who could lay claim to the title.

"There is no husband."

"Then what are you doing here?" the cabbie asks, the surprise evident in his voice.

What can I say to answer that question? The answer is obvious to me after a few seconds. "What am I doing here? I'm living. Turn to your left, right across from the university."

"You live back here? This place belongs to the family of..."

I cut him off. "I live here now. Please pull up to the front; someone will be out to get my bags."

At the sound of the car in the drive, Wilhelmina and Woapla come running out. Joseph comes from the side of the house and takes the luggage from the cab driver.

"Old ma, you came back!" the two young ladies cry as they race to hug me.

Joseph smiles and easily lifts my two bags. I pay the cabbie and watch him depart before turning to enter the house.

"Does the old man know you are coming?" Woapla says.

"My father knows where I am. Why?"

"No, no the Boku!" Joseph persists. "He has the key to the suite."

My hand goes into my bag and comes out with the key Alita had given me before." No need to trouble him. I have everything I need."

Willie and Woapla make an issue over what will be for supper and what to bring for me to drink. Once supper is settled, I go to my suite of rooms to unpack and put on clothing more suitable for the Liberian weather than an airplane ride.

I hear Weah before he comes in the house.

"What do you mean she is here? How did she get here? She cannot stay."

I smile; pretty sure it will be seconds before he storms into the private sitting room. I barely make it back and drape myself elegantly over the sofa before he enters. My pose would have done an actress like Bette Davis or Joan Crawford proud.

Weah comes to tower over me. "Why are you here? You have no right to be here this is not your place."

Steam from the sweat being evaporated by the heat of his anger is coming off his forehead.

I give an elegant shrug and start at his feet, to slowly work my eyes up his body. The seconds spent looking at the area south of his belt cause a definite growth to his manhood. By the time I reach his eyes, the veins in his neck are standing out.

"Let me see which question, if any, I am going to answer." I clip my words to show my displeasure, and then stand up to give myself height and courage.

"I am here because I can be. I have the right to be here as evidenced by the key I used to open the door. As to whose place this is, well. It's not yours."

"You have to leave."

"No, I plan on staying, at least for a while."

"How long?"

"Till it's time for me to go."

"You are a quee woman you have no reason to be here corrupting others, teaching them to whore themselves."

If he had slapped me in the face, I would not have been more shocked. The idea of me corrupting anyone, let alone teaching them to whore is as laughable as it is insulting.

"And just who am I corrupting? I've been here before and the world hasn't stopped turning. But would you like me to corrupt you?"

I smile seductively across at him and remember the voyeur show in Monaco. I wish I had on heels and some red nail polish. Her show was all about attitude, creating the scene. It can't be too hard.

"What would you pay for me to pleasure you?" is my question to him. "And I can assure you that it would indeed be a pleasure."

"I would never lay with you." The sizeable growth in the groin area is not in sync with the words coming out of his mouth.

"Of course you would, if I set the price right. But I should warn you, kissing costs extra."

"It's not good for you to be here. You are a distraction."

"You know what? I may just need to allow you to sleep with me so we can get the anger fuck out of the way. But before we do, we'll need to come, have an orgasm, in front of each other."

My short clipped tone changes. Desire for him is growing and it is reflected in my voice.

"Do you know there is nothing more intimate than seeing a person release? The moment when you are incapable of coherent thought, when you world centers on your release. You are vulnerable, open, and ready. I want to see you ready, exploding, coming."

Weah's body turns rigid by degrees as I speak. His eyes glaze and his breath goes neither in nor out.

"Yes, I'll have to consider that." My hands slip under my very impressive breasts and stroke them through the thin tie dye fabric of my dress. The extra pointy nipples come to attention, and my tongue comes out to wet my lips. I simply give him an Alita smile. One that promises much and denies nothing. "Mmmmm. What a purely decadent idea, but not today. It's too hot." I turn and slowly swing and sway my generous hips to the bedroom door before turning back to face him. He had not moved at all.

"How much?" comes out in a whisper.

His words stop my movement to the door. They turn me back to face him with the safety of the room between us.

"Silly man, I have money, I don't need or want yours."

"You said it would cost."

"And it will, but you can't pay me in money, that would be too easy. Easy things are not valued they are quickly discarded."

"What then. What would it cost?"

"It would cost you desire."

"Ridiculous. How can I pay you in desire?"

"I will watch as your desire grows and will see you as you wonder what it will feel like for me to take your manhood in my hand and stroke you."

I can see said manhood straining for the promises being made. His mouth parts and he is using his mouth to breathe, very shallowly breathe. His eyes are glued to my hands as they caress my bosom.

"Stop it. Do not touch yourself so."

"These are mine, I can touch them whenever and for as long as I desire. And when you have enough desire, I will let you touch them, feel their weight, and sample the nipple."

My fingers are stroking in a downward movement. I lift them toward him and see him lean forward even as he is mentally fighting the attraction. His eyes never leave my hands. I stop them from moving. I take my left hand down the front of my dress and stop at the apex of my thighs.

"When I decide to accept your payment I will allow your hands to touch my thighs, I will allow you into the secret folds found at the top of my legs. You will find moisture, warmth, and softness. You will dream about my thighs until you touch them, have them part for you, welcoming your entry."

"You are wrong," he whispers in a voice laden with as much passion as mine. "I will never pay." He declares what we both know is a lie without batting an eye.

"No? I think you will and you will pay gladly."

My right hand goes to my mouth. My finger traces first my upper lip and then the lower lip as his eyes scorch me from across the room.

"And then you will pay extra to kiss me, to allow your lips to touch mine and see if the promises I'm making are true. You will pay extra to kiss me and see if I can make you forget the world outside of my lips for the time we are together. You will pay extra to see if I can deliver what I promise you will be the best loving you have ever had or ever will have in your entire life."

"No" He croaks the word as his eyes remain on my finger at my mouth.

I wet the tip of the finger and both of my lips. The finger at my mouth rotates around the edges before I take it into my mouth slowly. I close my eyes as I push it in to the second digit and then slowly back it out.

I slip my hands under my very impressive breasts and stroke them. I part my legs and let my hands travel south and cause my dress to rise north. The only thing underneath is the strand of beads I had purchased on my previous visit.

When I open my eyes, Weah's eyes are not on my face. They are following the finger making its way closer and closer to the wetness of my core. When it slips inside, I hear and see him catch his breath. I remove the finger and bring it to my lips, rubbing moisture on my lips before tilting my head back and running my tongue across my lips.

"Close the door on your way out, I need some private time." I walk through the bedroom door.

The action must have been a signal for him to come back from his frozen state. The sound of footsteps crossing the room is instantaneous. There is no need to press my ear to the door to hear what he is doing.

"You have to leave. Nie Swa, you can't stay." He shouts close enough to the door to make me turn the lock. There's no point in being stupid.

Weah makes more angry noises this time in his dialect. Finally he storms from the room.

I stay in the bedroom and try to relax myself before unpacking more goods. I encounter and take out the one thing I promised to complete. The novel I had started writing two years earlier, part travel, part fiction, and all good. The work I had created that tells the tale of my time with Mr. M.O.P. Digging through my purse I finally find a pen. Further unpacking is put aside for now.

I review my writing, of a fifty year old woman who met a man on a plane. I look over the handwritten pages in the notebook and gather the voice recordings I had made. Pen poised over paper. I have a title for it now and no husband to scoff at my attempts. I prepare to finish my opus.

On the outside of the notebook I write the title: Finding Passion: Confessions of a Fifty-year Old Runaway." I smile at the memories as they flood my brain and the words running around in my head, daring me to capture them, perfect them and put them on paper. I open the notebook and on the inside cover I make a dedication. Pen touches paper and I am writing, embracing my passion. The first words, the dedication are easy to write.

To a muse,

For everything through lives and past lives.

See you next lifetime.

A whispered breeze touches my ears and ever so faintly I hear familiar laughter and "yessss".

The writing has my full attention and keeps me focused until there is a hesitant tapping on the door.

"Old ma, are you thirsty?" Wilhelmina's voice is hesitant.

"Oh yes" I answer coming to unlock the door.

"I did not know if you were asleep. Much time has passed and I thought you may be hungry and thirsty now."

"Yes sweetheart, I am extremely thirsty." A glance at the clock shows three hours have elapsed since my encounter with Weah. My body is drained, as if the writing has taken a physical. I stretch and sip on the juice of some fruit Wilhelmina brings in on a tray.

"Thank you sweetheart. I'll eat later."

"Yes ma'am." Her quiet disappearance allows me to refocus on what I had written.

After what seems like ten minutes, there is another knock. Wilhelmina must have dinner ready and waiting.

"Come on in. I'll be ready as soon as I finish this sentence. I say without looking up from my work."

Nothing, in response. She must be miffed to have been kept waiting. I look up see Weah in the doorway.

"What do you want? To tell me how much I need to leave? Or have you thought about the two of us together."

"I do not even dream of such a thing. You are a wicked woman."

"I'm not a wicked woman, I'm an honest one. And, you have thought of the two of us together, I can look at you and see you have."

His pants were doing nothing to hide his erection. He is made to fit snug inside of me. He follows my eyes to the bulge of his crotch.

"Yes, you've thought about what I've said and probably much, much, more." I look up at him to smile. "I think you have dreamed about us. You do know the thought, the dreams, are the prelude to the reality. And what a reality it will be."

"I stayed away from here because I want you to leave. I just came to tell you I don't want you here."

"Okay. You've told me what you have to say. I choose not to believe you."

Weah spins around on his heel and marches to the door. "No, I don't want you." he says.

"Oh but you do. You want me right here, right now. On the floor or against the wall. I can smell your desire."

"That is fantasy."

"The fantasy is your denial of the desire you feel for me. I make no secret of my desire for you."

"Never," he tells me in a weak voice. Then stronger as if trying to convince himself, "Never"

"Never doesn't exist for us. The only question is when."

The look on his face says everything. He stares unblinking, seeing what we both know.

"Now, I'll tell you. It's about the reality. Think about the reality of us and come back when you are man enough to face what the reality will be for both of us. Until then, leave me alone. I have work to do."

Without another word, he turns and leaves.

I go back to my writing, promising myself that in fifteen minutes I'll stop and eat. After ten minutes, I hear the door open again.

"I promise I'm coming Wilhelmina."

"I am not Wilhelmina."

"This is getting tiresome. Did you come with more commands for my departure Weah?"

"No I came back for the reality. I want the reality."

I stand and turn to him. I don't know where this will lead or how long it will last, but it's time to embrace this passion, welcome this adventure.

"Come to me."

THE CUSTOMS

The sharing of cola and pepper is a common occurrence in Maryland County, Liberia. I am often told the reasons for the ceremony since I am the outsider. It is a fascinating service and one that Marylanders strongly adhere to when strangers come to visit.

The practice of a false burial is common in the indigenous area of Maryland County. I have attended some of these ceremonies and was struck by the amount of detail and cultural identity that is put into the event. The timing of the false burial is generally a year after the individual's death. However, I had to alter the timing to fit my story.

The term Boku means old man and is used for family. Old Ma is what would be used for an older woman, similar to a grandmother and Auntie is used for an older woman, not quite family.

ABOUT THE AUTHOR

Christy Cumberlander Walker is the proud mother of seven children. As an empty nester, she decided to indulge in her passion and write novels. Christy recently relocated to Vegas and is enjoying the view of the mountains. She loves to talk about her novels and enjoys getting e-mail about her books.

She is currently working on her next project. Visit her website to see what is coming next.

Made in the USA
San Bernardino, CA
07 July 2014